Impact

By

Nate Johnson

Purple Herb Publishing

AuthorNateJo@gmail.com

https://www.facebook.com/AuthorNateJo/

Dedicated to
Dylan Snodgrass

Other books by Nate Johnson

Intrepid (Taurian Empire 1)

Blackthorn (Taurian Empire 2)

Discovery (Taurian Empire 3)

Drake's Rift (Taurian Empire 4)

Dauntless (Taurian Empire 5)

The End of Everything (The End of Everything 1)

The End of the Beginning (The End of Everything 2)

The End of an Era (The End of Everything 3)

The End of Hope (The End of Everything 4)

The End of the Road (The End of Everything 5)

The End of the Line (The End of Everything 6)

The End of the Chaos (The End of Everything 7)

Worth Saving (Post-Apocalyptic)

Impact (The End of Times 1)

Stolen Reality

Nolan Reed

A Demon's Nightmare

First (Short Story)

Chapter One

Ryan

They say a billion people died that first day. And yes, that is with a B. I sometimes think they were the lucky ones. It took another six months for the next billion to die.

Of course, I didn't know what was going to happen. I woke up that morning happy with life. It was spring break, and Dad was out of town doing his professor stuff down in California, my younger sister was visiting her friend in Oklahoma. I was on my own for three days. Come on, pretty cool for a seventeen-year-old.

Dad hadn't worried about leaving me alone. He knew there wouldn't be any wild parties. I didn't have enough friends to have a clique, let alone a crowd.

Feeling all adult and stuff, I made sure Jake our German Shepard was fed and watered. Got myself some corn flakes and plopped down in front of my computer to check out what was going on in the world. Or really, to see if anyone was online to play Skills of Death.

I'd just booted up when Dad called. Probably checking on me. "Hey Dad," I said as I continued to load the game.

"Blue Jester," my dad said.

My stomach fell. That was our family's code word. This was real, not a drill. Not a joke. Shut up and listen. All the danger things you grew up being afraid of were coming true. I being the tough guy, froze.

"You there son?" he asked.

"Yes, Sir," I answered. Like I said, this was serious.

He took a deep breath and said, "It's going to hit. The asteroid."

My heart stopped beating as I quickly started to search for news articles. This couldn't be happening. They'd said it would miss us. As if knowing what I was doing, Dad said, "They screwed up. I tried to tell them."

Things were happening too fast as my mind tried to comprehend. There was nothing new on the web. "But …"

"Listen, Ryan," he said. "They tried to push it away. Twice."

I'd heard about them thinking about using nuclear explosions. That was why Dad was down in California working at the Jet Propulsion Lab. It wasn't supposed to come too close, but they were looking at it as an experiment. Just in case a future asteroid or comet came too close.

"What do you mean?" I managed to get out.

"All they did was slow it down. It changed the trajectory. They don't have time to try again."

My stomach fell as I began to realize what this meant. Hey, my dad was an astrophysicist. I'd grown up with space being a constant topic around the dinner table.

"Are you sure?"

He scoffed. "It's math. Of course I'm sure. I wish I wasn't. You need to get out. My gut tells me this is going to hit in the Pacific..."

"Dad," I interrupted, not wanting to face what he was telling me. "I mean this is crazy."

"Just get out," he said, "Get to high ground. Real high ground. Then get to your grandfather's."

"Papa's?" I asked in disbelief. "His farm is in Idaho. You're okay with me driving all that way? Alone?"

There was a long pause, then he said. "You might have to walk."

"What?" I snapped.

"Listen. We've talked about this. These things might give off an EMP. We don't know for sure. But you know what that means."

"But, he's in Idaho. It'd take me years to get there."

"Weeks, if you focus. Grab your pack and every bit of food you can carry. Plan on camping. No electricity. No cars. No lights."

"Dad?" I said, unable to believe it. "What about you?"

"Don't worry about me. I will see you at your grandfather's."

My stomach clenched as I heard the doubt in his voice. He was a thousand miles away and the world was ending. "What about Cassie? Chase, Haley?" My cousins, Chase and Haley had lived with us until we moved to Seattle eight months earlier so Dad could teach at the university of Washington. The four of us had grown up together when my mom, aunt, and uncle had died in a car crash.

"I'll call the others," he said. "But you're first. You're in the most danger. The tsunamis will be huge."

A cold shiver shot down my spine. Dad didn't over-dramatize. "How huge."

"Think miles high. This thing is solid iron and two miles across."

"But ..." I mumbled. Unable to believe it. Unable to accept what I was hearing. Everything I had ever known was destroyed.

"Just get out," Dad said. "Grab what you need. And son, get my Baretta from the safe. You know the combo."

My entire body wanted to shake as adrenaline rushed through my system. This was Dad. He didn't scare but I could hear the terror in his voice. This was real.

"Okay, Dad," I said. What else could I say? My father was telling me that the world was about to end. Literally. A sense of purpose filled me. Get to Papa's. Live. "What about Cassie," I said. "Should I try to get her?"

"No," Dad snapped. "You get to Papa's. Your sister will have to get there on her own. You'd never get to Oklahoma. I'm going to call her and tell her to get to your grandfathers. You'd miss each other on the road."

His words made sense. But leaving my little sister was just wrong. Inside I determined to get to Papa's then head south to find her. A gut-churning worry filled me. At only a little over a year apart, we were close, especially after mom died.

"Listen, Ryan," Dad said, pulling me out of my wandering mind. "Just go, don't look back. Take what you can't live without because it won't be there to come back to."

Swallowing hard I nodded then remembered I was on my phone and said, "Yes, Sir."

"And, Son," he said with a heavy sigh, "Always know, I loved you. And I'm proud of you. Always was. A man couldn't ask for a better son."

My heart broke then I re-worked his words and realized he'd said, loved, as in the past tense. My father wasn't anticipating surviving through this.

"I love you too, Dad. I ..."

"I've got to go," he interrupted, "I've got to call the others."

And he was gone. I stood and looked down at my phone, wondering if that was the last time I would ever talk to my father. A numbness filled me as I fought to hold back a tear. I don't know how long I would have stood there but Jake nudged my leg. Obviously, my dog knew something was wrong and I needed to fix it.

"Okay, boy," I said as I stuffed my phone in my back pocket. "What do we need to survive the end of the world?"

Jake barked encouraging me to hurry.

It was like someone lit a firecracker under my butt. I rushed to grab my backcountry backpack out of my closet. I stuffed two sets of clothes and four pairs of socks into the bottom. Took my Papa's old military mess kit down off my shelf and shoved it in along with my emergency kit.

I'd made it in Cub Scouts years ago. A small plastic box with fishing line, hooks, Band-Aids, storm matches, three snare wires, two bullion cubes, and a decade-old starburst. The

13

kind of thing to get you through a night in the woods, not the end of the world.

"Okay," I said to Jake as I hurried into the garage and grabbed my sleeping bag and a four-person tent. The smallest we had. Next my gallon canteen, the kind with a strap for the shoulder. A flashlight and four D batteries still in the package. Then I remembered the most important item, a roll of toilet paper.

I ran to the kitchen, my heart racing. I hadn't asked Dad how long. An hour? A day? Ten minutes?

I mean the thing could be coming straight for me. A bullet with my name on it.

"It won't matter," I said to Jake. "I'll never know."

Jake's tail wagged in agreement as he followed close to my heels. Food. We still had four packs of freeze-dried camping food. We'd used it last summer for a camping trip. I stuffed the foiled packets down next to my clothes then rushed to the kitchen.

When I opened the pantry I froze. What did I take? I had minutes. Light, I realized, thinking of those freeze-dried packages. So I of course snatched every Top Ramen packet. All nine of them. Then a round box of oatmeal. A two-pound bag of rice and a box of spaghetti noodles. Then I grabbed the jar of bullion cubes and started to stuff it in when I thought that every little bit of weight mattered and just dumped the cubes into the pack and tossed the jar onto the counter.

Then I thought it through and grabbed the jar and filled it with Clorox, screwing the lid down tight. "Water purification," I said to Jake as I stuffed the small jar into my pack.

When Jack wove next to my leg, obviously worried, I remembered and said, "Yes, you too." So I got a large Ziplock bag and filled it with his dry dog food. "It won't last two weeks. We'll have to get you more on the way."

What else? I wondered as I stared at the pantry and everything I was leaving. My mind was flashing between ideas. What to take, hurry, this couldn't be happening, back to wondering what to take. Finally, I just gave up and slammed the pantry door.

I was halfway out the door when I remembered the gun. Rushing back to my Dad's room I opened the safe in the back of his closet and pulled out the 9 mm Baretta and a box of ammunition. My hand shook. This was getting serious.

Then I saw the stack of money, hundreds wrapped with a paper band that said $5000. Should I? Yes, I realized. Dad had said there would be nothing left. But still, it felt like I was stealing.

I stuffed the gun, ammo, and cash into my pack. Tied off the tent and sleeping bag then started for the front door but I was passing

Dad's library and slammed to a halt. All those books. He'd spent a lifetime collecting them. Everything on the stars. But he'd given Cassie and me our own shelves.

Stepping in I grabbed Heinlein's "The Moon is a Harsh Mistress." I know. Of all the books in the world. Why did I choose that one to survive the end of the world? Simple. Because my mom gave it to me.

"Can you think of anything else?" I asked Jake.

He just wagged his tail, thrilled that we were going on an adventure. Oh, God, if he only knew.

When we got to the pickup I opened the door for him to jump up then threw my pack into the back seat. I took a moment to gather myself. No use looking back, I thought. This wasn't home anyway. Dad and Cassie weren't there.

I was backing out of the driveway, all ready to race for the mountains when someone threw a monkey wrench into my plans.

Someone named, Kelsey Morgan. The goddess across the street.

A thousand thoughts flashed through my mind. Should I warn her? I mean, the girl hadn't said three words to me since we moved in eight months earlier. Of course, we ran in different crowds. Hers was the

Cheerleader/Jock group. Mine was the loner/outsider group. A group of one in fact.

But she needed to know. I slammed on the brakes and screeched to a halt.

She stood on her porch frowning at me. I knew that look. A jerk was going to hit on her. Why couldn't they know not to?

I swear, I was tempted to just keep on driving. But then I thought of that wall of water washing over her and just couldn't.

"Kelsey," I yelled as I jumped out of the truck. Her frown grew deeper. I could see her mind creating rejection lines. "I just heard from my dad, the asteroid is going to hit. We need to get out of here. Tsunamis, earthquakes, EMP."

Okay, not my best but I was sort of in a rush.

Her frown softened into a smirk and she said, "Ryan Conrad, that has to be the worst pick-up line in the history of boys."

I could only stare at her. It was like talking to a beautiful painting. No matter what I said, it wasn't going to make any difference. She had her mind made up. I wasn't worth believing.

"I'm serious," I said, unable to just walk away. "It's going to hit. Dad said all of this will be wiped out."

She didn't laugh but instead did what any girl would do and pulled out her phone.

Chapter Two

Kelsey

Eight months and the boy hadn't said a word to me. That whole mysterious loner thing. And now, here he's telling me the world was going to end. What kind of fool did he think I was"?

Ignoring him, I scrolled through my phone. "Nothing," I said without looking up then froze. A story about the president leaving suddenly on his helicopter. Someone saying there was a rumor about war, another saying it was the asteroid.

My stomach fell as I looked up and saw the seriousness in Ryan's eyes. This wasn't a joke. Not some way to mess with my mind. Besides, Ryan wasn't exactly known for his wild sense of humor or practical jokes. No, he was a serious one. Some might have said a stick in the mud.

But I'd watched him for eight months. Hey, he was a cute boy who lived across the street. Of course I kept an eye on him. Like I said, a loner. Never joined any of the groups. The kind of guy just marking time until he could graduate.

"I'm serious," he snapped. "I can't waste time trying to convince you. If you're coming, let's go."

No way this was real. But deep in my stomach, I felt a sense of doubt. Swallowing hard I continued to scroll trying to find something. Anything that could tell me what to do. Then I clicked on a link at JPL. Even I knew of that place. A blog came up. Some guy named Keith talking about how people at JPL were scrambling to get out. How the parking lot was cleared in a dozen minutes.

This was real, I realized. "Let me get my stuff," I said before I thought it through. Yes, I was being an idiot. This couldn't be happening. But another part of me was saying it was. To many coincidences.

He sighed heavily then said, "Get clothes, dry food, I'll get my dad's pack."

I stood there watching him run back to his garage, and yes, my jaw was hanging open like a beached fish. Finally, I shook myself and rushed inside. Clothes he said. What did a girl wear to the end of the world?

Jeans, socks, T-shirts. And underclothes, I wasn't going through the end of the world all skanky.

The front door opened and he rushed in, no knock, obviously, manners were taking a back seat. He held the bag open and I stuffed my clothes in. A rolled-up sleeping bag was tied to the bottom of the pack.

His brow furrowed as he looked around the room then grabbed my boots from the bottom of my closet and a winter jacket.

"Why?" I asked.

He ignored me, shoving them into my arms then rushing to the kitchen. "Here," he said as he started handing me stuff from the pantry. I didn't really pay attention and just shoved them into the backpack.

I swear it wasn't more than two minutes since he stopped his truck and now we were running from the house like thieves in the night. The unrealness hit me. I was jumping into a truck with Ryan Conrad to run away from the end of the world.

His dog stuck his head between the front seats and sniffed at me.

"Jake, this is Kelsey," Ryan said as he started his truck.

"High Jake," I said as I let him sniff the back of my hand then ruffled his fur. Have I told you that I am a pushover for cute dogs? And it said something that Ryan had a dog. I don't know what it said, but something. I mean serial killers didn't have dogs. It was a well-known fact.

"Buckle up," he said then threw the truck into gear and floored it.

"Hey, slow down," I yelled as I fought to get my seatbelt done. "You'll end up killing us before we get there."

He shot me a scowl and didn't let up, swerving around the corner, only slowing down before running a stop sign.

"I'm serious Ryan,"

He let out a long breath through clenched teeth and said, "Dad didn't say how long we have. It could be minutes."

"How bad could it be?" I asked.

He turned another corner, I swear the two tires on my side lifted up off the road.

"Think dinosaur killer. In that league."

My stomach clenched. No, this was impossible. A numbness filled me as I tried to think. No, impossible. Suddenly I thought of Mom. Scrambling, I pulled my phone out of my back pocket and called her. Each ring on the other end was like a knife to the stomach. "Please," I prayed.

Finally, on the fourth ring, my Mom answered, "Kelsey?"

"Where are you, Mom?"

There was a heavy sigh on the other end. "I told you. I flew to Spokane this morning for a conference. I'll be home late."

A sense of relief. "Stay there Mom," I said.

"Kelsey, what is going on."

A new fear filled me. My mom was never going to believe me. But I had to keep her in

Spokane, it was the other side of the mountains. "Mom, the asteroid is going to hit."

"Kelsey," she said with an exasperated sigh, obviously thinking I was being over dramatic. Suddenly Ryan indicated I should put it on speaker.

"Mom, Ryan Conrad is taking me. We're going to the mountains." She sort of had a thing for Professor Conrad. When they moved in she must have taken them casseroles a dozen times. Then a few weeks later she sort of stopped. When I asked why she'd said sadly, "He's still in love with his dead wife."

"Kelsey," My mom gasped, "What is going on? Ryan Conrad? You said he was weird."

My stomach fell, my mother said those words moments after I had put her on speaker. My face grew warm with embarrassment.

"Mom …"

"Mrs. Morgan," Ryan said as he swerved around a Honda civic. "My father is down in California, working on the team monitoring the asteroid. He said it is going to hit, probably in the Pacific."

There was a long pause and I knew my mom was fighting to not believe. "Is he sure?"

Ryan scoffed, "It's math, he's never wrong. And he doesn't freak easily."

24

"Mom," I interjected, trying to add to the argument. "There's strange stories on the internet. I think it's going to happen."

Again there was a long pause. Finally, she said, "Get to the mountains. I'll rent a car and start for you. Maybe I can get a flight."

"No," Ryan suddenly said, "We'll miss each other. And flying might not work. Stay in Spokane. We'll come to you. Where are you staying."

"The Davenport," That was my mom, first class when it was on her company's dime. "But..."

"This is best, Mrs. Morgan," Ryan said as he looked over his shoulder to merge with the traffic on I-90.

My mother surprised me as I heard the tears in her voice, "You take care of my little girl. Do you promise?"

"Yes, Ma'am," he said as if he made such promises every day.

"I mean it Ryan Conrad, if anything happens to her I will haunt you for the rest of your life."

He swallowed hard, shifted lanes, then said, "I promise."

My insides sort of stiffened, "Hey, I can take care of myself." I swear, if he had laughed I would have punched him.

"Call me," My mom said, "I've got to tell the people here. But call me in ten minutes."

"Okay,"

"And Kelsey," she said again with that tear in her voice. "I love you, honey."

"I love you too Mom. We'll be alright, I promise." Oh, how wrong can a girl be?

My heart broke and I had to fight to not start crying. This was all too much. I was about to ask Ryan what he thought was going to happen when he suddenly swerved around traffic and I had to grab the dashboard.

"Jesus," I cursed. "You're going to kill us."

He ignored me, his eyes focused on the road. Swerving around slower vehicles.

Taking a deep breath I looked out at Lake Washington as we crossed the floating bridge. Picturesque sailboats, and in the distance a float plane touching down. All these people didn't know what was going to happen.

Was he wrong? Oh, please be wrong. But deep in my soul, I knew he wasn't. What was going to happen? Would we get away? What then? A thousand thoughts flashed through my mind as I tried to get a handle on it.

I cracked the window and took in a deep breath, trying to calm my racing heart. The air had that typical Northwest smell of pine and salt. "This is impossible," I muttered, mostly to myself.

"I wish," Ryan said as he clenched his jaw.

News! I needed information. I turned on the radio while I pulled out my phone and started scrolling. The radio was tuned to a classic rock station. I glanced over at Ryan and lifted an eyebrow.

He shrugged.

Shaking my head at his choice of music I started scanning the dial until I heard the word, Impact. Freezing, I leaned forward to listen.

"... I repeat, we are receiving word that the Asteroid might come closer than originally thought. It might even skip off the atmosphere..."

Ryan scoffed.

"... In fact," the voice continued. "You may wish to go outside, if it gets close enough there will be a beautiful light show, even in the day, the biggest shooting star you will ever see."

"How long?" Ryan mumbled.

"How long until it is here," Another voice asked.

"Five minutes," the announcer said.

"Jesus," Ryan yelled as he stomped on the gas.

I grabbed the handhold and braced against his seat, wedging myself in the corner to stop from flopping around. Ryan jerked the wheel and tore around a semi. My heart raced as I looked down at the speedometer and saw it cresting above ninety.

"Maybe it will miss us," I said. "If it does and you get us killed. We'll be the only casualties from an asteroid that never hit us."

Again he ignored me as we rushed through the Eastgate suburbs. McMansions filled with Microsoft employees. Looking over my shoulder, I could still see Seattle in the distance. Suddenly the sky exploded with light, like a second sun had filled the atmosphere.

I winced and looked away, my eyes burning.

Ryan cursed as he started to slow down.

"What are you doing" I yelled. Seconds before he had been racing like a bat out of hell and now he was slowing down.

He looked over at me with sad eyes and shook his head while pumping the breaks.

My heart stopped as I suddenly realized the engine wasn't racing like it had seconds before. He was fighting with the steering wheel as the car slowly bumped along the concrete barriers then back into the lane. Finally coming to a halt on the shoulder.

"EMP," he whispered with disbelief.

"What?" I gasped. I think I knew, but I didn't want to admit it. Then I saw that all the other cars were stopped, and my heart fell.

"Electrical Magnetic Pulse," he said then paused before continuing. "Dad thought this might happen. Something that big, made of iron, hitting our atmosphere at those speeds. It's like an atomic bomb going off."

I stared at him, trying to work out what that meant. As if seeing my confusion he continued, "Basically electricity and anything that runs on electricity is done. Switches, chips, burned out."

"For how long?" I asked.

He shook his head, "Forever. Or until we can rebuild an industrial complex, all without power. Think back to Civil War days."

Suddenly a heavy boom rocked the truck. Jake whined and dipped his head in pain. I held my breath as the deep sound washed through me.

The sound was followed by a shock wave that almost tipped the truck over. Screaming I grabbed Ryan.

He pulled me close as we held each other while the truck was bounced across the road. Then it was gone as if it had never been there. But I knew the truth, Ryan had been right. My world was about to end.

Chapter Three

Ryan

Dad had been right. I know, stupid thought, but I couldn't not feel a sense of pride. Dad had been right. I suddenly realized I was holding Kelsey Morgan. A fact that I might have imagined a time or two thousand but never thought would come to pass.

Suddenly I remembered what was happening and backed away. "We need to go." I was out the door and pulling on my pack when she looked across the back of the truck like a little girl, terrified at her new reality.

"Come on," I said in my best reassuring voice. "We've still got time."

She didn't look like she believed me.

"Put your boots on," I told her, "And strap your coat over the top of the pack."

She continued to stare at me, a numbness in her eyes.

"Kelsey," I said in a firm voice. "Just do it."

She shook her head then started moving. A minute later she stood up and slipped the pack over her shoulders and buckled the belly strap. I put the leash on Jake and started east. He was voice-trained, I'd spent two years at it. But he was as scared as I was and I didn't need him running off.

People were getting out of their cars, looking up at the sky then at each other with a dazed expression. A car breaking down was understandable. All of them breaking at the same time didn't compute.

Leaning forward, I focused. I pulled out my phone to get the time but it was dead. A sickness filled me as I realized all we had lost. Get her to safety. Get to Papa's, Get my sister. Those where my thoughts over and over.

We hadn't gone a hundred yards when I noticed a van with a mom and four kids in the back. The look of worry on her face hit me. More people who needed to be rescued. I knocked on the window. She jumped then stared for a second before opening the door.

"Get to high ground," I told her. "We need to worry about tsunamis."

Her brow furrowed, "We're six miles from Puget Sound."

"We're not far enough," I said, adjusted my straps, and started forward. I didn't have time to convince her.

Kelsey jogged to catch up with me then glanced over her shoulder.

"We don't have time," I said to her.

The look of pain and disgust in her eyes made me flinch but I didn't stop. I had to live. My sister would need me. Besides, I'd promised Mrs. Morgan I'd protect Kelsey. But my gut still churned every time we passed people. We'd tell them to get to high ground then keep on walking. I soothed my aching soul by telling myself that I had warned them. It was up to them to do it or not.

We were about a mile from the breakdown, just stepping onto an overpass when Jake suddenly began whining and barking at the same time while pulling at his leash. Three seagulls jumped into the air and started cawing at each other. I froze trying to identify the danger then realized what was happening and pulled Kelsey back off the overpass.

Her face scrunched up in anger as she took a deep breath to yell at me when the biggest earthquake in human history hit. Like someone had pulled a rug out from under us. She screamed as I dropped to the ground, making sure she fell on top of me just as the rolling and shaking began.

"Hold on," I yelled. The roar was like a freight train hitting a mountainside at full bore. Wave after wave threw us into the air then dropped out from beneath us, each time slapping us with hard concrete.

Every fault must have let go at the same time.

Kelsye screamed.

I held her, trying to keep myself between her and the hard ground. "We'll be okay," I screamed trying to reassure her and myself. We were outside, away from buildings.

Suddenly the world tipped to the side and we started to slide only to be thrown back. And still, the ground rumbled. Spitting and jumping like an angry bull trying to throw us off his back. I forgot to breath as I felt as if everything I ever knew had disappeared.

Still, it rolled. Would it ever stop? Oh, please, I begged, just make it stop. My body ached and my heart raced with pure terror.

Again we were lifted up into the air like we were on a trampoline only to fall back down. The air was knocked out of me when Kelsey's elbow connected to my gut. And still, the ground shook.

Two minutes, that was how long I think it lasted. I would have said two hours, but I was trying to be realistic. Finally, the rolling slowed, not as extreme, until it became a gentle shudder then nothing.

An eerie silence fell over the world. A smell of dust tickled my throat as I fought to gather myself.

"We're alive," Kelsey said in obvious surprise.

"For now," I said as I stared up at the sky. "What do you think? Ten minutes since the asteroid hit? Maybe twelve. My phone isn't telling time."

She frowned then shrugged.

"Good, that gives us a couple of hours until the wave."

Her frown deepened as if she didn't understand.

"Shock waves travel through rock at about seven thousand miles an hour. Twelve minutes means about a thousand miles away. A wave travels about five hundred miles an hour through water, which means two hours. We need to hurry."

"How do you know that?" she asked not with doubt, but shock.

I wanted to say, doesn't everyone? But stopped myself, "I just do. Come on."

She stood up dusting off the back of her pants then froze. I followed her gaze and groaned. The overpass had collapsed. My gut lurched. Five more feet and we'd be down there mixed up in a pile of rocks.

Swallowing hard, I took a moment and started to examine our surroundings.

The highway was passing through a suburb. Houses were flat, and watermains had erupted shooting streams of water into the air. Suddenly something exploded, making me duck. It looked like a gas main had been set off with a line of fire shooting off at a forty-five-degree angle. The only reason there weren't more was because the electricity was dead.

Shaking my head, I tried to push it all out of my mind. We needed to get out of there.

"Come on," I said as I approached the edge of the collapsed bridge slanting down to the street below.

Kelsey joined me then said, "Aren't we far enough away yet?"

"Best case scenario maybe. Worst case, no way."

She swallowed hard then sat down, put her feet over the edge before pushing off and sliding down the concrete. When she touched bottom she looked back up at me, silently asking what was taking me so long.

I quickly joined her then helped her up the far side. And no, I didn't have to push her butt to get her up over the edge. We had just reached the top when the ground began to shake again. Kelsey screamed as I pulled her down to the ground, but it suddenly stopped. Teasing us with death.

"Let's go," I said when I realized we weren't going to get hit again.

It took us another hour to go three miles. Weaving our way through tumbled cars and around jack-knifed semis. Twice we stopped to help pull people out of crumpled cars. But I refused to stay. Once we were sure they were out I let other people worry about them and pushed Kelsey to keep going.

She would always shoot me a doubtful look, but she didn't fight me. I think the reality was starting to set in, we moved or we died.

There were so many weird things it was hard to take it all in. The dust. The Pacific Northwest isn't known for dust. The shaking had thrown the dust into the air. At the same time, the sky looked the same as always except with a heavy haze. But I think the weirdest was the silence. No sirens. No helicopters racing to rescue people. A woman crying echoed down the road, nothing competing to be heard.

When we turned a bend in the road I froze. Two things hit me at once. One, the town of Issaquah looked like Godzilla had thrown a temper tantrum. And beyond it, the Cascades and our safety.

Kelsey stood with her hands on her hips trying to catch her breath. I could see the shock and pain in her eyes. Reality was finally hitting us. Everything had happened so fast, but now, this. We couldn't pretend it was just us. That it could be fixed and we could go back to our life.

And this wasn't the worst that was going to happen I thought as I touched Kelsey's back and nodded that we needed to keep going.

She wiped at a tear then glared at me, daring me to say anything about it. I ignored her, patted Jake, and started. We needed to get to the foothills at least.

The sun beat down, the pack's straps ate into my shoulders, and I could feel the beginning of a blister but we couldn't stop and rest.

Luckily we were on I-90. A modern freeway above most of the destruction. Sure it was mangled and cracked with steel guardrails twisted into pretzels. But it wasn't the local roads. They looked worse with houses or what used to be houses sitting in the middle of roads. Trees and telephone polls intercrossed so badly that a tank couldn't have gotten through.

People on the side roads covered in dirt and dust walked in a daze. Blood and open wounds. But I ignored them and kept pushing.

Twice more we had to climb down then up collapsed overpasses. Another time a bridge had pancaked, blocking our path, but being on foot it only took a minute to scramble over it and keep going.

As we walked, I kept glancing over at Kelsey. Her pretty face was covered in dust, her hands looked red and torn. No longer the pretty princess who ruled our school. The girl that every other girl wished she could be. Popular and liked, and yes, those are different things. Beautiful and smart. A cheerleader without being stuck-up.

And now she was running for her life. I'm sure not what she expected this morning.

Seeing me checking her out she shot me a quick look, "What?"

I laughed and shook my head, "I'm sure this wasn't how you planned to spend your day."

She just frowned at me.

Suddenly something hit me. "Hey, what about Troy? You didn't call him?"

Glaring at me she shook her head, "That is because Troy Hamilton is a cheating, controlling bastard with the morals of a sick alligator and the brains of an onion."

I winced, okay, do not make this chick mad. She knew how to carry a grudge.

"Besides," she continued. "He would have been too dumb to listen to anything anyway."

Okay, she didn't think much of Troy Hamilton. A thought that sort of made me smile. "When did you guys break up?"

Her frown shifted. "You really are out of touch, aren't you? I thought the whole school knew. A month ago. It was sort of public, in the lunch room. Not one of my finer moments. But that is what happens when your boyfriend accidentally sends you pictures of him in bed with your best friend."

I ate my lunch in the computer lab so I might have missed that. Besides I didn't spend a lot of time talking about Kelsey Morgan.

Suddenly we were hit with another small tremor that reminded us about what we should be doing. Without a word, we both started hurrying.

It was a half hour before we saw our first dead body. That surprised me until I realized that the highway was open not much to fall on people. People shouldn't have been hurt that bad. We'd gotten through it with bumps and bruises. Although my back felt like an elephant had tap danced all over it.

A car had been turned on its side trapping a man. His cold stare told me he was dead. That and the two thousand pound car sitting on his chest.

Kelsey shivered and looked away.

I cringed and thought what was truly remarkable was the lack of response. No ambulance. No firemen with jaws of life. Just people moving down the road in a haze. Ignoring the body. Some going back to Seattle. Others, like us, trying to get away. And too many standing around without a clue.

How many others were out there, I wondered?

We'd just reached the top of the first foothill on the far side of Issaquah when a cold shiver shot down my spine. Taking a deep breath I turned to look behind me and froze.

Kelsey turned to join me and whimpered. There in the far distance, the horizon was slowly changing. A gray wall was replacing everything, slowly moving towards us. A wall of water. So large that I could easily see it at ten miles.

"No," Kelsey gasped.

We should go, I thought as my heart began to race. But my legs were frozen. This was unbelievable, everything disappeared into the gray wall. A wall that towered a mile above the highest skyscraper.

The few people around us began to scream and run but I knew it was either too late or we would be fine. A hundred yards wasn't going to make a difference.

Besides this needed to be witnessed. The people in its path deserved that. Suddenly I thought about that mother and four children and wanted to cry. No way they had gotten away.

Without thinking, I took Kelsey's hand in mine and held on. And yes, if you had told me that morning that I would spend my afternoon holding Kelsey Morgan's hand watching a mile-high wall of water race towards us I would have known you were crazy.

The giant wave broke, tumbling over itself, rushing towards us.

"It's getting smaller," Kelsey said, perhaps with more hope than certainty.

But she was right, the more it advanced the shorter it became, a half mile. A quarter then eventually only a hundred yards tall. Eight miles from the distant shore it became a wave and stopped being a wall.

At ten miles it was a rushing river a hundred miles wide. Eventually, we saw it rushing down streets with the houses being torn from their foundations and subsumed.

We stood there frozen watching the water slow until there was only a trickle.

"We're alive," Kelsey said.

I laughed, "How many times are we going to say that today?"

She didn't answer but continued to watch. All of western Washington had become a lake. A lake filled with debris and bodies.

"It's gone," she gasped. "Everything."

I could only swallow. She was right, everything between us and Puget Sound was buried in water. And when it pulled back there would be nothing but scoured earth. Hundreds of square miles of nothing but mud. No buildings, no trees, no roads, no people.

Chapter Four

Kelsey

My body went numb. My mind floated in nothingness. It was too much. All I could do was stand there and look at the end of my world. Everything I had ever known was gone. Home, friends, all of it gone.

I didn't cry, I was too numb to cry, but I knew that this moment would never leave me. That I would always carry it.

"Come on," Ryan said as he gently pulled at my hand. "We need to keep moving."

"What now?" I snapped. "What is going to try to kill us next?"

He grimaced then shook his head. "I need to get you to your mom and I need to get to my Papa's before I try to find my sister."

His words didn't register. There was too much. It was all just too much. I wanted to fall down and curl into a ball. Pretend it was all a dream and wait for things to go back to the way they were before.

But he was insistent and kept pulling at me. Then Jake nuzzled my other hand, telling me to listen to his master.

Sighing, I nodded and started walking. I didn't know where. I didn't even care. It was just putting one foot in front of the other, going where Ryan led.

"I'd be dead," I whispered.

"What?"

"I would have died if you hadn't stopped. If I hadn't stepped out the front door when you were leaving I would be dead."

He winced.

"I mean it," I insisted. "A few seconds either way and I would be dead. I was going to Krissy Jensen's. We were going to work on a new routine." Suddenly it hit me. Krissy was dead. Everyone was dead.

I lost it and started to cry. I pulled my hand out of his and fell to my knees crying.

Ryan stood there with a face in obvious pain. Guys so hate to see a girl cry. They are lost. All I wanted him to do was hold me. Promise me that everything would be okay. But he stood there like a stump until I was able to pull myself together.

He's right, I realized. We need to keep moving and I was also positive he was regretting being stuck with a sniveling girl. The last thing he needed was more problems.

Sniffling, I pulled myself together then stood up and started walking, adjusting my pack, determined to get to Mom. She would know what to do.

He hurried after me, shooting me quick looks, probably terrified I was going to break down again. I gave him a weak smile trying to reassure him.

"What is going to happen?" I asked him. Partly because I wanted to know and partly because I just wanted to talk and that was a question that he couldn't ignore. I knew he'd have it already mapped out.

He surprised me by shrugging. "It depends."

"Don't do that." I snapped and instantly regretted it. It seemed I had fallen into the habit of speaking without thinking things through. I took a deep breath. "I'm sorry, but people always say that. Give me your best guess."

"If you mean us? We get to Spokane, find your mom. Then I go to my Papa's farm in upstate Idaho. If you mean the world …"

His pause ate at my soul. He didn't want to tell me how bad it was going to be.

"I would guess that every coastal city was hit by that tidal wave. Even over on the Atlantic side. It won't be as big, but because all communication is wiped out no one will get any warning. And most people in the world live within ten miles of the ocean.

"What else?"

"Storms, flooding, maybe volcanoes. More earthquakes."

My heart hitched as I thought about the death and destruction. "And then?"

He glanced over at me and shook his head. "The only reason we got to eight billion people is because we can move food from where it's grown to where people live. We can't do that now."

"So," I said as we wove around two cars wrapped around each other. "Destruction, famine, pestilence, and death. A lot of death."

He only nodded, obviously not wanting to talk about it. But I needed to know, a desperate need to understand so I could have some concept. My world had disappeared. I needed to start building a new one.

An anger began to grow inside of me. I grabbed ahold of it and held on, knowing I would need that anger to survive. "What about the military?"

He shrugged again. I was really getting tired of that shrug. "The Navy is gone. Most of the army stuff isn't shielded. Besides, most of it relies upon civilian stuff, oil, industrial complex, and stuff like that. I wouldn't expect them to do much. They're mechanized, and that stuff doesn't work anymore."

A silence fell over us as I took it all in and tried to come up with a plan. Some way to make it all better.

We passed other people. Most of them in a daze. Some sitting by the side of the road looking like they'd been hit by a train, staring off into the distance, unable to believe what they were living through.

And still, we walked. My legs were beginning to ache and the pack was biting into my shoulders when Ryan suddenly stopped and pointed. "We need to get off the road and set up for the night."

I frowned at him then looked up and realized the sun was an hour from setting. My stomach rumbled and I realized we hadn't eaten all day. Then it hit me. I'd be spending the night in a tent with a strange boy.

It's amazing, the world ended and I was worried about something so silly. But that didn't ease my concern. And no, I wasn't worried about Ryan. The boy put the name to Boy Scout. I knew the type, strong, loyal, a gentleman. No, it was something else that I couldn't put my finger on.

He led us down an off-ramp to a side road. The telephone poles were down and wires lay across the street. He saw me flinch away and said, "No power. Don't worry about them."

I felt like an idiot but I still made sure to step way over them.

About a quarter mile off I-90, he helped me climb over a wooden fence so we could take a trail.

"Where are we going?" I asked.".

He shot me a quick frown. "I'm looking for a place where a fire can't be seen. Someplace that the smoke can be hidden through the trees."

"Why?"

He suddenly stopped and turned to face me. "Listen, Kelsey, the rules are different now."

I frowned back at him, upset because he wasn't making sense.

Sighing, he rolled his eyes. "You're a girl." He said as if that explained everything.

"Yeah. So?"

"There is no one to call for help. No one to stop people from taking what they want. And you're a pretty girl." He stopped, looking at me until what he was saying began to sink in.

"People aren't like that."

He scoffed and shook his head. "You know perfectly well they are. Or at least some of them. And it only takes a few to ruin your life. So the best thing to do is be invisible. Especially at night."

Turning, he started back up the trail. I hurried after him taking in his words and realizing he was being protective and I needed to get my head out of my butt. He was right. The world was run by new rules and the quicker I adjusted the longer I might live.

After a few minutes, he found a group of boulders where we could make a fire that couldn't be seen from the road. Jake made a quick circuit sniffing to make sure everything made sense then turned and wagged his tail as if giving his approval.

Ryan sighed as he slowly lowered his pack off his shoulders. I saw him wince and knew it was more than just carrying a pack all day.

"You're hurt."

He grimaced and then gave me that patented shrug. "Yeah, someone landed on me just as I fell a dozen feet onto concrete."

A guilt filled me as I remembered during the earthquake him twisting, placing himself between me and the ground.

"Come on, help me with the tent."

We had it up in ten minutes. I could tell he knew what he was doing. It was obvious that he had been camping. Something I had never done. I'd grown up with an absent father and a mother who hated the outdoors, who said the only good camping was a hotel with hot water and deep baths.

I watched him move as he went about making camp, gathering wood, pulling a hatchet from the side of his pack before stashing both packs in the tent. A small sense of security filled me as I realized just how lucky I was. Not only being alive. But being with Ryan. Almost every boy at school would have been a lost cause. Ryan just seemed to know what he was doing. Everything from avoiding asteroids to building campfires.

Within minutes he had a fire going and a pot sitting on two rocks waiting to boil.

"Have a seat," he said as he pointed to a log six feet from the fire. "This will take a minute."

I sat down and watched him work. He caught me looking then said with a small smile, "Don't expect the royal treatment every day. Your life as Princess Kelsey is over. You get to make breakfast."

"Princess Kelsey?" I asked, offended and sort of pleased. "Is that what you thought of me?"

He frowned. "No, I sort of figured that was what you thought of yourself."

Okay, fully offended. "Hey. I wasn't like that."

He laughed, a laugh that hurt me. Then he saw my scowl and shrugged. "Tell me you weren't the prettiest girl in school. Head cheerleader. Boyfriend, correction, former boyfriend football captain. Homecoming queen. A cheerleading scholarship to UW next year. Destined to marry a doctor or lawyer, a good-looking one. Or become one yourself. In my world, that is as close to princess as you can get."

49

My stomach clenched. Did people really think I was like that? All surface stuff. They didn't think about growing up without a father in my life. The constant worrying about my grades, about making sure I never upset anyone. Constantly being judged. All they saw was what I let them see, never the fear eating me up inside.

"But," he said after pouring the contents of a Top Ramen pack into the pot. "At least you were a benevolent Princess. You weren't one of those cruel ones."

"What about you?" I snapped. "Mr. Mysterious. The proverbial loaner. You never joined us. Looking at the world like we were all beneath you. Like you had everything all figured out and you weren't going to share the secret with the rest of us mere mortals.

His brow furrowed for a second then he laughed. "What? You mean spend my time getting drunk on Saturday nights with people who wouldn't know what is important if it bit them in the butt."

"What is important then?" I asked with bitterness.

"Ah, that is the question, isn't it? I don't know. But I know what it isn't."

"And now," I snapped, suddenly angry. "All that sad loner stuff. Well, at least you didn't lose any friends today."

He winced then said with the saddest eyes ever. "No real friends. Just my father."

Chapter Five

Ryan

At least she had the grace to flinch when I said I had lost my father. That was one thing about Kelsey, she did have class.

I pushed aside thoughts I shouldn't be having and tried to figure out the future. Tomorrow, the day after, a week, months, years. All of it looked dark and dangerous.

We sat there for a moment, silently eating the Top Ramen. I was about half done when I gave Jake the rest of mine then grabbed my pack from the tent and pulled out my dad's pistol, double checking to make sure there wasn't a round in the chamber. I'd wait until I needed it before I jacked one into the barrel. Yes, a risk, waiting, but a trade-off. I didn't need to have the thing going off when I didn't want it to.

"What's that?" Kelsey gasped.

I frowned at her as I shoved it into my belt, "Most people call them guns."

She glared at me and said, "I don't know if I'm comfortable with you having a gun."

Laughing, I shook my head. "If we need it, you'll become comfortable real fast."

Her frown deepened then she said, "Why are you mad at me? I didn't cause all this."

My heart fell. She was right, I was taking out my anger on her. I was furious at the world. I was angry that I was alive and Dad probably wasn't. I was mad that my sister wasn't where I could save her. These and a thousand other worries gnawed at my gut.

"I'm sorry," I said as I started emptying out the packs.

"What are you doing?"

"Confirming what we have, seeing how much food we have."

She lifted an eyebrow when I finished.

"Four days worth," I said, two people went through stuff twice as fast. I should have grabbed more. But five minutes later and we would have been caught by that wave. "We'll need to get more. Maybe tomorrow."

Turning my back, I removed five hundred dollars from the bundle and shoved them in my pocket, and stuffed the rest back down into the bottom of my pack.

"We should probably get settled, it will be dark soon. Go ahead and make a trip to the bushes."

She frowned at me like I was speaking Greek then the realization hit her. She glanced at the forest then back at me in complete shock. I just shrugged. Like I thought, princess. She'd probably never gone camping in her life.

Jake was kind enough to go with her and they both came back a few minutes later. She gave me a look that could have boiled water at a dozen paces but I just ignored her as I held the flap open for her to get in.

As she crawled into my dad's sleeping bag I placed the hatchet just inside the door and pulled the pistol from my belt and put it down next to the top of the sleeping bag.

"Roll up your jacket," I told her, "For a pillow." I then turned my back and slowly worked off my flannel shirt. I'd sleep in my jeans.

"Ryan," Kelsey gasped.

"What?"

"Your back. It's all blue and yellow."

Sighing I sat down and started to pull off my boots. "Yeah, it gets that way when elephants stomp on it."

"Are you alright? It looks like it hurts."

"I'll live," I mumbled as I slid into my bag. Leaving unsaid the fact that so many other people wouldn't be able to say the same thing that night.

A sadness hit me as reality began to sink in. We were in trouble. Not just Kelsey and me. But people in general. I knew deep in my gut, things were going to get so much worse before they got better.

Reaching out, I ruffled Jake's neck. He'd settled in between the two of us. I smiled at him and silently thanked him for being with me. I swear he understood. His soulful eyes looked back at me and said he felt the same way.

A hint of vanilla and coconut hit me and I realized it was Kelsey's shampoo. God, even after the end of the world and I felt lost thinking about her.

Sighing to myself, I turned over and tried to pretend she wasn't sleeping two feet from me. Surprisingly, I didn't toss and turn. I didn't lay there thinking about how terrible my life was. I was out in thirteen seconds. It had been a long day.

A jay singing just outside the tent woke me. A persistent cry that couldn't be ignored. That and nature calling got me moving. My body was stiffer than a seasoned Four x Eight. I swear I had to consciously force my muscles to work and I knew they would scream in pain every time I moved.

A faint gray morning light filled the tent. Glancing over I saw Kelsey lying there, her hands folded under her head, looking at me with wide eyes.

"Morning Princess."

She sort of smiled back at me. "Five minutes,"

I laughed, my sister would say that whenever Dad woke her for school. My heart hitched, Please, I begged, be alright Cassie. Don't do anything dumb.

We grabbed a quick breakfast of oatmeal. And no, I didn't make Kelsey cook it. She would have been lost. But I did see that she followed me and watched as I got the fire going. And she did have to clean up the pot and dishes.

When we were all packed up I winced as I slipped into the backpack. She touched my arm and said with a concerned look. "Is there anything I can do?"

Shaking my head, I bit down on my back teeth and forced myself to start moving. "I'll be okay," I lied.

The sun had just peaked over the mountains when we reached I-90. The air smelled of pine and future rain. I suddenly froze as I looked up the highway and then back from the way we had come.

"What?" Kelsey asked.

"People," I mumbled. "Everyone is gone."

She confirmed what I was saying then shrugged. "They're probably not morning people like you."

I laughed and started walking east. The sooner we got to Spokane the sooner I could get to Papa's. Kelsey fell in with me. One thing I had to give her. She didn't complain. I knew this was unusual for her. Living rough. But she wasn't bitching. That was major points in my book.

"Listen," I said. "North Bend should be coming up. It's a big town, they should have supermarkets. You stick close."

"Yes sir," she said as she shot me a smirk.

"I'm serious."

"I know you are," she said, "you are always serious."

That stung a little but I ignored her and focused on moving forward.

When we got to North Bend I had to stop for a moment and get my bearings. The town didn't look as bad as Issaquah, but not much better. Houses were down, cars stuck in the middle of the street. Trees lying with their roots exposed. But there was enough openness so we could get through.

My stomach clenched when I thought about what we might find as we got deeper into the town. An eerie silence engulfed us and I wondered where everyone was at. I was beginning to get worried they'd all disappeared then I heard yelling in the distance.

I glanced over at Kelsey, then Jake. My dog's neck fur was on end. That was angry yelling. "Come on," I said as I began to hurry. The yelling grew louder until we got to a Safeway. The windows were broken and people were running out of the dark building carrying things.

Freezing I looked around, there were no cops. No angry store owner with a shotgun.

"They're looting," Kelsey said in surprise.

"One day," I said as I shook my head. "People weren't ready for this."

"What are we going to do?"

"Join them," I said as I started for the store.

"Ryan," she hissed.

I ignored her, waving for her to hurry up and stick close. "We need food. I'll pay for it."

She shot me a doubtful look but she stayed even with me. My heart raced, But still I hesitated. This was wrong but necessary. What would Dad say to do? That was my mantra. I needed to survive and we needed more food if I was going to make northern Idaho.

When we got to the door I paused, peeking inside. A dark cavern greeted me with fleeting figures dipping in and out of shadows. The faint reek of spoiled food hit me. I knew it would get so much worse over the next few days.

Someone inside yelled and a fist hit skin followed by a whimper.

"Stay close," I said as I pulled out my flashlight and stepped over the broken glass threshold. Kelsey grabbed the back of my shirt. Jake growled letting me know we were stepping into danger.

I paused, getting my bearings then went to one of the checkout lanes and grabbed some plastic bags. "We only get things we can carry. Light, high in calories."

She swallowed hard and nodded.

I swept the flashlight back and forth. People looked at me. Some with looks of guilt. Others with insane eyes daring me to challenge them. I cataloged the dangerous ones and maneuvered Kelsey away from them until I found what I was looking for.

Half the packages of beef jerky, A bag of flour, another of sugar, a small bottle of olive oil, Two bags of hard candy, a dozen packets of gravy mix, and more Top Ramen. When the bags were all full I started Kelsey for the front door. Holding my breath we could get out without anyone stopping us.

Where were the store employees, I wondered then realized they were either home with their families or joining us looters. When we passed through the checkout line I tossed two one hundred dollar bills on the conveyer belt then pushed at Kelsey's back to get her going.

Just before we stepped outside I had her hold up as I scanned the parking lot. No. Nobody was going to shoot us for looting.

"Come on," I said as I stepped out into the sunshine, scrunching up, expecting a bullet to rip through me at any moment. Thankfully nothing tore through my chest. Only when we made the main road was I able to breathe.

"We made it," Kelsey said then shot me a big smile at her words. Words she had said too many times in two days.

"For now," I said as my stomach fell. Four guys were moving in. I could see it in their eyes. We were prey. We had the two most valuable things in the world. Food, and a female.

Jake growled and pulled at his leash. I held tight and kept moving forward, hoping they would change their mind. But of course, we weren't so lucky.

"Hey," the taller one said as two slipped around behind us.

They looked like they'd fallen off a hay wagon. Country boys. Flannel shirts, cowboy boots. Early twenties. Their world had changed and they were going to take advantage.

"Thanks for shopping for us," the tall guy said with a heavy smirk. "We'll take the bags and your packs. You ain't from around here. That's our food."

I glanced over my shoulder. The two behind us were holding back. They were new to this, I realized. Their first robbery and I could see hesitancy in their looks at each

60

other. Unable to believe they were actually doing this.

It was the tall guy pushing them I realized. When he looked at Kelsey and licked his lip I realized I only had one choice. I dropped the bags of groceries and pulled the pistol and shoved a round into the chamber with a loud click. "Is it worth dying for?" I asked him.

The color dropped from his face. He hadn't expected me to be armed. I mean a ton of people around her carried firearms. But they'd pegged us as from the city.

"Grab the bags," I told Kelsey without taking my eyes off the tall one. Then over my shoulder, I said, "You two move, and your friend dies."

The tall guy swallowed hard, not taking his eyes off my gun.

The four of them froze in place, unsure of what to do next. I nudged Kelsey with my shoulder to walk around them and kept my gun trained on them as we passed them. "You've got a hundred other people to go after. You leave us alone and I'll forget all about this."

The tall guy glared at me, but I could see his mind working. I was right. There were other, easier targets out there.

Turning, I walked backwards, keeping them in sight until we were far enough away so that I could breathe again.

Glancing over I saw Kelsey's fight face look back at me with eyes wide. "We're not in Kansas anymore, Toto."

I laughed, wow. The princess was tougher than she looked.

Chapter Six

Kelsey

My heart refused to settle down. Ryan had pulled that gun so quickly. So easily. And I had seen it in his eyes. He'd been willing to shoot. Thankfully, the other guy had seen that same look and backed down.

Everything was so messed up. It was like being on ice. One false step and I'd end up falling on my butt. And just when you started to think you had discovered all you needed to know. Someone tipped the ice and you had to figure it all out again.

Ryan kept glancing over his shoulder to make sure we weren't being followed. We were a quarter mile down the road before I saw his shoulders relax as he stuffed the pistol into his waistband.

A new awareness hit me. I was walking down the middle of a road with a boy armed to the teeth. I had just looted a store. I would never go home again. And the only thing between me and a hideous future was this boy.

"What do you think are our chances?" I asked him. "Making it to Spokane." Suddenly I was desperate to know.

He thought for a long moment then shrugged and said, "Maybe seventy percent."

My heart fell. That meant we would die three out of ten times. In normal times it would have been one in ten million.

We continued on as I thought over this new idea. It was amazing. I had almost been killed three times in the last day. I knew how easy it would be. Ryan's numbers didn't seem far off.

"Hold up," Ryan said as he let out a long breath and dropped his pack to start loading it with stuff from the store. When he had me do the same I winced, the pack was getting heavy. That made me smile. I had thought I was in shape. You had to be to be a cheerleader. It wasn't just looking good. But aerials and cartwheels didn't prepare a girl for walking twenty miles with a heavy pack.

We were almost out of town when Ryan suddenly turned towards a strip mall. I frowned as I rushed to keep up. "What?"

He nodded to a pawn shop with an old bearded man standing at the door with a shotgun cradled in his arms.

Ryan held up his empty hands and yelled, "You open?"

The old man studied us for a minute then said, "Ain't got any guns. Sold out yesterday in two hours."

Ryan sighed, obviously upset then asked, "How about jewelry? Gold chains?"

65

I glanced over at Ryan trying to understand. The man's brow furrowed then he nodded, "Yeah, got some." He looked us over, obviously wondering if he could trust us then shrugged, "Drop your packs and come on,"

A storm lantern sat on the display case, the yellow flame throwing a sallow light over the store. Ryan handed me Jake's leash then started examining some cheap gold chains.

"Ryan," I said, "those aren't pure gold."

"They're gold enough," he said without looking at me then asked the man how much for a handful of gold chains. They bantered back and forth until they agreed to three thousand dollars. I gasped. He really was going to do this.

"Throw in some snips, and you've got a deal."

The man looked shocked but simply raised an eyebrow and pointed to a section of tools. Ryan grabbed a pair of snips then pulled out a wad of cash from his pocket and counted out thirty hundred dollar bills.

I put a hand on his arm trying to warn him but he shot me a nasty look that told me to back off. I gulped and stepped back then decided if he wanted to be an idiot he could do it on his own and took Jake outside.

Ryan joined me, stuffing the chains into a side pocket of his pack then winced when he pulled it on over his shoulders.

"Why?" I asked, unable to keep my mouth shut. It just didn't make sense. And where did a boy like Ryan get that money?

He let out a long sigh then said, "Money isn't going to be worth anything." He then glanced over at me and added, "I'm sorry for snapping at you. But I didn't want him thinking things through."

"What do you mean? Money is not worth anything"

"it's just paper," he said. "It's only good because everyone accepts it as a way to pay for things. But everyone's bank account is gone. All those electrons were fried. The government isn't working. So what do people trust? Gold."

For the thousandth time, my stomach clenched. Was he right? Before I could ask, he added, "The snips are for cutting off links to pay for things."

My brow furrowed, the boy thought of everything. What kind of person did that make him? A planner? Smart? Or had he just read about all this in some book?

We continued up I-90. The road was starting to climb the mountains and we had to lean into our packs. My calves were burning and I was having to fight not to beg to stop and rest. But the air smelled of pine trees. A gray day. A typical Northwest spring day.

Thankfully, about three miles out of town, we found a rest stop. One of those places for people to pull in and hit the bathroom, stretch their legs. The place was eerily quiet.

"What happened to all the people?" I asked waving at the cars in the parking lot.

"I bet most of them walked down to North Bend yesterday. It's easier going downhill than up."

A shiver ran down my spine as I thought about everyone unable to get home. What about Mom? What would she do when we found her? Where would we go? Ryan had his grandfather's farm. But Mom and me?

We sat at a picnic table and shared a bag of beef jerky. When we were done, Ryan filled his canteen from a faucet that still worked and motioned it was time to get on the road.

Once again we fell into silence as we walked, each lost in our own world. After an hour I just couldn't take it anymore so I asked, "Why were you such a loner?"

I know, sometimes words come out of my mouth before I think.

He shot me a quizzical look then shook his head, "I was pissed off, I guess."

"Why?" I asked, surprised at his answer.

"Stuff."

"No, don't do that. What stuff?"

He took a deep breath then said, "Let's see. My mom died six years ago. I've been pretty furious ever since. Then my dad got the job at the University of Washington. We had to move from Tulsa to Seattle for my senior year of high school."

I cringed inside imagining leaving all my friends.

"Plus," he continued. "My cousins who had lived with us since the car wreck. The one that killed my mom and my aunt and uncle. They decided they didn't want to come to Seattle. Chase was eighteen and took off. I think he's working on a fire crew down in California. Haley is going to a fancy art school in New York city."

"Were you guys close?"

He was silent for a moment but I saw his jaw tense then he said, "Chase was like my big brother. And Haley and I were in the same classes at school. And she was a godsend for Cassie. The four of us were real tight. We'd spend every summer up at Papa's farm. So yes, we were tight."

My stomach churned. I had been an only child. No cousins. Just Mom and me against the world. I'd always been jealous of my friends who had brothers and sisters. Then I realized he had no idea what was going on with his family. I at least knew Mom was alright.

Yeah, I guess I could understand why a boy might be stand offish. He was only going to be there for a year. And why get close to people when you're just going to leave?

We once again fell into a silence as I thought about him and his world. Suddenly he said, "So, what were your plans? I mean, what does a princess do after high school?"

The way he said princess made my shoulders hunch, finally though I dismissed it and said, "I was going to go to the University of Washington. Hey, I might have had a class with your dad. What about you?"

"Central Washing, over in Ellensburg. They've got a world-class geology department."

"Geology? Rocks? Why am I not surprised." Then it hit me, of course, that was why he knew that stuff about earthquakes. He was a rock nerd. Also, no people so no drama, no loss.

He shrugged.

Funny, he didn't look like a geologist. I remembered how he'd pulled that gun. No, he acted more like a soldier or a cowboy from the old west.

We continued on. Twice we saw people walking down on the other side of the highway. Once they waved but no one stopped. People were already getting leery of strangers. We continued up. Always up.

Weaving around abandoned cars and the occasional semi.

We passed through the town of Tanner and I was wondering when we would stop for the night. Last night, in the tent, had been weird. A strange boy was sleeping only a few feet away. What if I did something in my sleep? Snored? Burped? Something to embarrass me for the rest of my life.

Of course, I'd been so tired and the day so terrible that I fell into a deep sleep, obviously trying to hide and forget about all the dreadful things that day. We'd have to do it again tonight. In some ways, it was even worse. I knew him now. Or at least the part of him he allowed to be seen.

"Are you hungry?" I asked, silently hoping he'd get the hint and stop for the night. My legs were beginning to get numb.

He glanced over at me then said, "Yes," and then continued walking.

Jesus, the boy could be denser than one of his rocks.

I was just about to come right out and ask him to stop when he froze. I followed his gaze and gasped. A mountain had come down and buried the road. I mean, this wasn't a mud slide. This was half the mountain, rocks, and trees all mixed up together blocking both sides of the road.

But then I saw three kids sitting on the guard rail behind an SUV. Two girls and a boy, about thirteen, in middle school would be my guess. The boy raised his hand then quickly dropped it when one of the girls punched him in the arm.

"Hey," Ryan said, as his eyes scanned the area looking for danger signs.

The boy pushed up off the guard rail and approached. "It's blocked."

Ryan nodded as he looked across the pile of rocks. It must have been forty feet high and stretched from the hill across the road meeting the slide from the other side.

"You guys all alone?" Ryan asked, obviously curious as to why three young teenagers were out here all alone.

The boy swallowed hard, "We were coming back from Seattle, the state science fair."

I swear he was almost embarrassed saying it. The two girls got up and joined him.

"Where's your teacher?" Ryan asked as he twisted to make sure no one was coming up behind us.

The boy pointed east. My brow furrowed until I realized he wasn't pointing east, he was pointing to the pile of rocks.

"The car stopped. They all stopped," the boy said. "I think it was an EMP. Mrs. Harrison was walking to find help when the earthquake hit. She was … buried."

The look of pain in his eyes tugged at my heart. Both of the girls looked like they were going to cry. The taller, thicker one had purple hair, but she still looked like she was going to melt down.

"I'm Paul," the boy said. "this is my sister Julia," he said, pointing to the mousy one. "And that's Tania."

Ryan's jaw clenched as he studied them for a moment then the pile of rocks blocking our path.

"We were headed home, to Cheney," Julia said with obvious worry. "Do you know what happened?"

"Asteroid hit," Ryan said as he started walking towards the pile.

"Ryan," I hissed. "You can't leave them here."

He stopped and I swear he wanted to shoot me, but he sighed and looked back at them. "We're headed to Spokane, you're welcome to tag along."

The boy Paul frowned, "You're not supposed to leave a spot. You're supposed to wait and be rescued. It's easier for them to find you."

Ryan shook his head. "No one is coming. Seattle is gone, power and cars are off line and aren't coming back. It's all gone."

The color drained from their faces as the truth began to sink in.

Ryan sighed heavily then said, "Grab your stuff, any food, blankets, clothes, and let's go. We need to cross over before it gets dark."

My stomach dropped as I realized Ryan planned on climbing the rock slide.

"But …" Paul said.

"Your choice," Ryan said then turned and started mapping out a route up and over the blockage.

The three kids huddled up, arguing in hushed tones. I hurried up to Ryan and grabbed his arm to stop him. "We have to wait. We can't abandon them."

He glared at me for a moment then shook his head. "You really do think I am an unfeeling beast, don't you? I'm just giving them time to realize the obvious. There isn't anything to argue about. They just need to accept it and we don't have time to coddle them. But this means we're going to be even shorter on food. I think we just dropped below fifty percent whether we make it or not.

One in two. A flip of the coin. My stomach fell, was I signing our death warrant by making him take the kids?

Chapter Seven

Ryan

My gut churned. Three kids. No way this worked out right. But Kelsey was correct, I couldn't abandon them. Dad would have been pissed at me.

Leaning down, I unclipped Jake's leash and started up the rock slide. Jake and the others would have to find their own way up and over. I'd try to find the easiest way, blaze a path. But they were going to have to climb themselves.

I used a branch buried in the rocks and mud to pull myself up and over a large rock then felt it shift under me and realized the whole thing could come down. It was nothing but a loose pile of debris. But I pushed on, my feet sinking into mud searching for purchase. Twice I felt my pack pulling me backwards and had to scramble for a hand hold. But finally, I made the top and could see a clear road up ahead.

"Hey," I called back to them. "If you're coming. Let's go. It's going to get dark soon."

Kelsey shot me an evil glare then took a deep breath and started up. The others had grabbed what looked like school backpacks from the SUV. You know the kind used for books and supplies. I'd check them later to see what we had to add to the lager. Now, I needed to get them up and over.

76

I watched as Kelsey reached out to pull herself up. The girl was athletic without being hard. That feminine sporty look that was just so hot. She glanced up and caught me staring. "What?" she yelled.

Laughing, I reached down a hand. She grabbed it and let me pull her up to the top.

I stayed there and helped the other three up and over. Then the five of us worked our way down. When we reached the bottom I passed around the canteen then got them started on the road.

We traveled the next quarter mile in silence. Each lost in our own world. I knew what the kids were thinking. Who was this guy and could he be trusted? The Paul guy kept shooting me frowns and always placed himself between me and his sister.

Good, I thought, the kids had a head on his shoulders.

We were working around a tanker when I saw an old pick-up with a tarp covering a bed full of firewood. "What an idiot," I mumbled to myself and detoured to start taking the tarp.

"You can't do that," Julia said with a frown.

I shot Kelsey a look thinking about our looting then continued untying the tarp. "They aren't going to need it. In fact, we should be searching every car. Both sides of the highway.

Food, blankets, clothes, water. Anything we might need camping."

"Camping?" Paul asked.

As I rolled up the tarp I tied it off over the top of my pack then swung it up on my shoulders.

"Figure two weeks. We need food and stuff to stay warm. There isn't going to be any hotels."

"Why not?" Tania said. "There is a town about every twenty miles. If we time it right we can be in a motel every night."

Stopping, I started to explain the new facts of life, but Kelsey saved me. "Because we need to avoid people."

Three frowns responded to her.

She took a deep breath and explained what we had already seen. The looting, the attempted robbery. "And it's only gong to get worse. So we camp, hide. It's our best hope of getting there."

All three of the kids still looked doubtful but Kelsey smiled at them and said, "We girls will take the other side. You guys take this. Ryan is right, we need to gather up everything we can find. Think of it as free shopping."

"Take Jake with you," I said, "And keep even."

She took Jake's leash then nodded for the girls to join her.

Paul continued to doubt me but he helped me look in each car. We got into a routine. I'd put my hands over the window and look inside. The third car had a blanket on the back seat but the doors were locked. So I pulled out the hatchet and used it to break in.

The shattering of glass echoed off the mountains like an alarm telling the word, 'Thief'.

At first, Paul hesitated but the next truck had a jackpot. Paul pulled himself up and looked in the sleeper cab and yelled. "food."

"What?"

He leaned down and said, "Power bars. The protein kind. And two blankets. Also a bottle of whiskey."

"Get it all," I said, "We can trade the whiskey."

I helped him load my pack then we continued on. We were slowing down, I realized. Going up hill and spending time to search we weren't going to get as far as I hoped. I looked over at Kelsey and sighed. She was keeping even, her and the others jumping from car to car.

Jake shot me a look telling me he was making sure everyone was alright.

"So," I said to Paul, "Science Fair. What, the state championship?"

He blushed and looked down. "I know, not super cool. But ..."

I laughed, thirteen-year-old boys hated being thought of as not cool. "Hey," I said. "it beats sitting home playing video games all day."

His blush grew deeper and I knew I'd unintentionally hit a sore spot.

"That's my vice," I told him. "Too much time wasted, my Dad says."

His eyes lit up and we spent the next twenty minutes talking video games. The kid was smart I realized. His observations about some of the games were spot on and you don't go to state Science Fair unless you're semi-intelligent.

As we continued searching we found two water bottles, a bag of cloth diapers I made him take, and a grocery bag filled with kitchen cleaner stuff.

"I wished it had been frozen Pizzas," Paul said as he put it back into the car.

I laughed then felt a cool breeze on my back. I turned to check it out and froze. A black cloud was coming in from the west. Not just a cloud, but a wall of cloud. The kind that back in Oklahoma, we would have called tornado weather.

"Kelsey," I yelled then pointed. Even at fifty yards, I saw the color drain from her face when she saw what was coming our way.

"Come on," I yelled to Paul as we rushed across the median to the girls.

"What should we do?" Kelsey asked as she looked around for an escape.

"We batten down the hatches," I said to her as I passed and started into the forest. My heart raced. We didn't have time. But I needed to make sure I picked the right spot. We were going to have a biblical storm. We needed somewhere that wasn't going to flood. And that wasn't going to slide down a mountain.

The river was on the other side of the far road. This side had an open spot without any mountain cliffs in dangerous territory. "Hurry," I yelled as I pointed to where I wanted the tent.

Suddenly the breeze picked up. Jake barked a warning, and the others started scrambling to get the tent up.

I broke tree limbs and laid them diagonally over a large log, three feet from the tent.

"What are you doing?" Kelsey asked looking up from shoving a tent pole into its holder.

"That's a four-man tent, which means it's a tight squeeze for three. We can't all sleep in there. Jake and I will sleep out here in a lean-to."

Here eyes grew big as she stared at me then at the wall of blackness coming towards us. I ignored her as I broke out the tarp and laid it over the branches then tied it off and anchored it with large rocks.

Kelsey looked at the lean-to and shook her head, I didn't know if it was admiration or disgust but when large raindrops started to plop on the forest floor she shuddered and hurriedly got the others and the packs into the tent. Just as she reached back to zip it shut she looked out at me with sad eyes.

My heart hitched, I didn't like the idea of leaving them. But they were only three feet away. It wasn't like I was abandoning them. Suddenly the thought of leaving Kelsey felt impossible.

"Yell if you need me," I said to her over the rising wind.

She smiled weakly then zipped the tent closed.

I got down on my hands and knees to roll out the sleeping bag then crawled in and called Jake to me. He curled up next to me shivering, hating what was coming. And boy did it come. I swear it was like someone pointed a firehose at my lean-to.

The air exploded with a thunder clap to let us know the storm had arrived. I wrapped an arm around Jake and pulled him close. I'd blocked off one end with my pack and the other was blocked by the corner of the tarp.

I'd chosen a north-south log to block the winds coming from the west and had tied everything down tight. But it felt wrong to be leaving Kelsey and the others. I pulled the tarp back to look at the tent only to be met with a wall of water.

The few large raindrops had been a tease. This was a deluge. A gazillion gallons of water had been vaporized when the asteroid hit. It all had to go somewhere and it appeared it had chosen our campsite to return to earth.

I knew this was happening everywhere on the west coast. But it felt personal. Like everything we did was useless because the universe was going to continue to try and kill us until it succeeded.

The wind grew stronger, picking and plucking at the tarp. I scrunched down in my sleeping bag and tried to pretend it was just a regular storm. But it wasn't. Lightening flashed and the ground shook with each thunder clap.

How long? I wondered, remembering the earthquake. Had it only been two days earlier? Suddenly my tarp was pulled by the wind and opened on the end letting in enough water to drown a frog. I had to scramble out of my bag to tie it off, getting drenched.

It was unbelievable the amount of rain. I tried to do some math but realized I'd never work it out. Too many unknowns. But a two-mile wide piece of metal had hit the ocean at tens of thousands of miles an hour. It must have put up so much water. The edges had probably fallen back to earth the first day. But everything else had been turned into steam. That had taken two days to gather, form as rain, and hit these mountains just as it was ready to let go.

"Ryan?" Kelsey yelled over the wind.

"What?" I yelled back as I scrambled out of my bag.

"I just wanted to make sure you were alright."

Sighing, I slumped down back into the bag. "Yeah, I'm fine. Jake and I are playing chess. He's winning."

She laughed and I knew all was right with the world. Or at least as right as it could be.

And still, it rained. The dark grew darker as night took over. And still, it rained. In bands. Hard for a few minutes followed by even harder. The lean-to was on a small slope. At first, a trickle of water worked its way in but eventually, it became a steady stream.

I worked on making a coffer dam to divert the waster around the opening. It helped but every two hours I had to scope up more dirt and push it into the opening.

Twice I pulled back the tarp to check on the tent but it had gotten so dark I couldn't see anything. There was just the howling wind and the constant pounding of the rain. Not that gentle patter. But a pounding. As if the storm wanted to physically hurt the earth.

Somehow I finally fell asleep only to waken in the morning with the continuing rain and a trickle of water seeping into my bag sending a shiver through my body.

"Why didn't you wake me?" I teasingly said to Jake. He looked back at me like I was an idiot. He was stuck outside the bag, why should I be comfortable?

I quickly rebuilt the dam then felt my stomach clench in hunger. God, I wanted a hot meal. My body felt drained, and weak.

"Why not," I said to Jake then smiled to myself. It wasn't that hard. I got my hatchet and cut a bunch of wood from the underside of the log. It was dry and would burn great. I used my buck knife to shave some splinters and got a fire going, pushing my pack back to create an opening for a chimney.

I had to scrunch down but I could almost sit up in the lean-to. Once the fire was going I put two pots outside for water. It took less than a minute for both to be filled to the brim. I tossed in a double handful of rice in one and some beef jerky in the other.

Once the beef jerky was softened, I added two packets of gravy mix, let it thicken, then set it aside to wait for the rice. When things were ready I called across to the tent. "Hey, Kelsey, you guys awake."

There was stirring then Kelsy yelled back, "You didn't wash away."

I laughed, the girl was tougher than most. "If you're hungry, make room and I'll be right over. Consider it breakfast in bed."

Suddenly there was a lot more shuffling and the sound of the zipper being pulled down. "We're ready."

I covered the food, grabbed the two spoons, then pulled my jacket tight and hunched my shoulders while waiting for a break in the rain. But it didn't let up so I took a deep breath before Jake and I and hurried across to the tent.

They were all sitting cross-legged, their backs to the tent wall. Kelsey smiled welcomingly then said, "You mentioned something about food. I didn't realize almost everything is in your pack. At least the good stuff."

She zipped the tent closed then smiled. "But we've got the candles, but no matches. We need to be more organized for the next disaster."

The teasing in her voice made me relax. If she was giving me a hard time then she was all right.

Chapter Eight

Kelsey

My stomach grumbled at the savory smell of breakfast. Ryan shot me a smile then passed me the spoon and took the top off his food. I took a spoonful of rice, dipped it in the gravy then moaned, it tasted so good.

We had to pass the spoon and pot around the circle, each taking a bit and passing it on.

"So, how did you guys sleep?" Ryan asked.

I shrugged. I'd unzipped my sleeping bag all the way and laid it across the tent floor. We had five blankets and a beach towel. At first, there had been some bickering about who would sleep where. I had insisted on being close to the door just in case Ryan needed me. Paul had insisted on sleeping on the far end. His way of being chivalrous. Julia had refused to sleep next to her brother so Tania had blushed while rolling her eyes.

I smiled when I thought about waking that morning and finding her arm draped over Paul soaking up his warmth.

"Fine," I said to Ryan without telling him I'd barely slept all night. I hate storms. But what was surprising was how much I had worried about Ryan.

I mean, a couple of things. This was Ryan Conrad. I barely knew him. And, this was Ryan

Conrad, the guy could handle just about anything.

"How long do you think this will last?" Tania asked him after finishing her bite.

Ryan took a deep breath and said, "Forty days and forty nights would be my guess."

The others blanched until they saw his teasing smile. "Two, three days at the worst. At least the first one."

They relaxed but Julia was squirming and I knew her problem. The bushes were calling. But we'd be drenched.

We finished the food and Ryan put the pots out to fill with water. We'd clean them later. So we sat there looking at each other, no one wanting to mention what was bothering them until Paul finally said, "I can't take it anymore and shot through the door and out into the woods."

Staring at him, we paused for a moment then all joined him, each going off in our own direction. Even Jake. In under the trees wasn't too bad. But getting there and back was terrible. The rain hit us like a garden hose at full force and we were drenched instantly. But a body has got to do what a body has got to do.

When we got back to the tent we were each soaked, our hair dripping water, our clothes sticking to our skin. I started shivering and knew I was going to come down with a cold. I always did when I got wet.

Thankfully, Paul pulled out a pack of cloth diapers and handed them out. But I was just too wet to make any difference. Swallowing hard I said, "I need to change or I'll freeze to death."

Paul's eyes lit up with that creepy thirteen-year-old smile at the thought of seeing a naked girl.

Ryan had the grace to not make a joke and turned his back then punched Paul in the shoulder to get him to do the same thing. They turned around and we three girls scrambled through our packs for new clothes.

Have you ever tried to change in a four-man tent filled with five people and a dog? It isn't easy. I mean pulling jeans on over wet legs is hard enough, but try doing it while you keep an eye on two boys to make sure they don't turn around.

After half of forever, we finally got into dry clothes and I felt my world start to feel better. Neither Paul nor Ryan wanted to change. I didn't know if it was because they just didn't want to appear weak, or if there was some other reason. Boys are weird that way.

We sat and talked, sharing our life stories. Ryan made the kids unload their packs to see what we had. Nothing but two sets of clothes each. The jeans and tops they were wearing and a pair of khaki pants and white shirt they'd worn during their presentation. A light jacket, and dress shoes.

Ryan tossed the dress shoes out of the tent. "No need to carry them." The kids gasped but didn't complain.

"Okay," Ryan said with a shake of his head. "We didn't find much food. We're going to have to cut back. Two meals a day. Maybe we can find more when we pass through towns or at the ski lodges on the summit.

We fell into a long silence as each of us thought about the long walk in front of us. Weeks with little food, dangers along the way, and an unknown future awaiting us when we got there.

And still, it rained. Later that afternoon Ryan and Jake returned to his lean-to. He tossed me the box of Power bars then closed his flap and disappeared. My heart hurt. He was just so distant. So all alone. He didn't need anyone, I realized. A guy totally comfortable with himself. It was enough to make a girl worry about things.

I'll admit it. I'm used to male attention. Every since I was Julia's age, guys had been chasing me. But Ryan was different. Like I said, concerning.

The next morning I woke to a strange sound. It took me a moment to realize it was silence. The rain had stopped. Sighing with relief I stuck my head out of the tent and looked up. The sky was still gray and menacing. But it didn't look terrifying, just the normal bad.

Ryan pulled back the tarp's flap and glanced at the sky then smiled at me. "I think we need to get going."

My stomach turned over. "What if it starts again?"

He shrugged, "We'll hole up in a car or something. We could have done that yesterday but I was worried about tornados. But it probably would have been smarter."

"What about breakfast?"

"We'll eat on the road. I want to make the summit before dark."

"Okay, give us a minute and we'll pack up.

Thirty minutes later we stepped out of the forest onto the highway. Things had changed. One, the river on the far side was up and over its banks, spreading across the far lanes. Trees were down with broken limbs scattered across the road. Plus, several cars had been shifted, the strong wind and rushing water pushing them sideways.

Ryan just shook his head, bent into his pack, and led the way East, up hill. As we walked I opened his pack and grabbed a couple packs of beef jerky. Passing them out I made sure everyone got equal amounts.

Twice the sky threatened to open up but both times the rain stopped almost before it started. My body was stiff from three nights of sleeping on the ground, my back ached from the pack pulling at it. And my calves burned from walking uphill. But Ryan didn't stop so I didn't either.

Several times we had to work our way up into the forest to get around the swollen river. When we came to an overpass that spanned the river we had to stop. The river had taken out the span on the left and pushed debris and logs into the right bridge, backing water up enough to flow over the top.

Ryan made us stop then got the tarp rope and tied himself off, handing me the loose end.

"This is stupid," I said to him as I looked down at the rope in my hands. What did he expect, me and the others to pull him to safety if the river took his legs out from beneath him?

He just laughed and turned to start making his way across.

I quickly got the others on the rope and gently plaid it out as my heart beat in my chest. The water rushed against his legs, mid-calf. He slowly took a step, then another, inching his way across.

I was freaking out. My hands had to gently let the rope go, I just wanted to yell at him to come back. But I knew Ryan Conrad by now and knew he'd never listen to me.

When he reached the middle he stumbled just a little and I sort of screamed in the back of my throat. He steadied himself then looked back and shot me a smile. I swear the boy was enjoying himself.

An anger shot through me. How could he do this to me? Yes, I was aware that we needed to make progress. Needed to get to my mom. But he shouldn't be risking himself like this.

But, as usual, he was right and made the far end.

"Okay, Julia next," he yelled, "Wrap your wrist through the rope and slide it along. You'll be fine. Slide your feet along the road. Don't pick them up. Keep as much weight as possible on the road."

She swallowed hard but I had to give her credit. She started out, following Ryan's instructions. I was finally able to breath when she made the far end and fell into Ryan's arms.

Tania was next, she made it almost look easy, and two people had shown her how to do it. When she made the other side she didn't even hug Ryan or Julia, just turned and said, "It's easy."

Yeah, right.

"You next," Paul said.

I balked, I was the older one. I should be last.

"Please," he said and I could see the need to be manly in his eyes. I was going to push back but then realized the last person could tie the rope around themselves and would be safer. So I nodded then took a deep breath and started out.

I was almost halfway across when Ryan suddenly yelled and pointed. My heart froze, a log was breaking loose and coming over the top of the bridge. Freezing, I waited to let it go in front of me. And everything would have been fine except the darn thing had a long branch still attached and that branch stuck up into the air just enough to catch the rope and pull me off my feet.

The sky tipped as I felt myself plunk into the river being dragged to the edge of the bridge. My wrist burned where the rope tore at the skin. The pack pulled me down, shoving my head under and I swallowed half the Snoqualmie River and knew without a doubt that I was going to die. Only to feel strong arms pull me up to fresh air.

Ryan had me, holding me up, blocking the river while pulling the rope free of the branch.

I sucked in air like a steam engine as I clung to him, terrified I would be swept away.

"Come on," he said as his arm wrapped around my waist steadying me.

I clung to him like a literal life line, my wrist felt all wrenched but I didn't care. All I wanted was to get out of there before something tried to kill me again.

The girls had the rope on one end, Paul on the other. My soul sent out a silent thank you. If either side had let go, I would have been washed away and ended up in what was left of Puget Sound fifty miles down river.

When I got to dry land I collapsed to my knees as my body shook. Ryan put his arm around my shoulder, just holding me until I got it all out. Only when I was able to breath again did I look up at him and say, "Next time, I go first."

He laughed then nodded for Paul. The boy tied the rope around his waist but didn't have any problems getting across.

Once everyone was safe, Ryan examined my wrist then used his knife to cut long strips from a T-Shirt and wrap in in a figure eight. "I don't think it's broken."

I just watched his hands gently take care of me and so desperately wanted to just sink into him. To have him hold me. Have him tell me everything would be alright. To feel that safe secure feeling his arms gave me.

But I'm not an idiot and stopped from making a fool of myself.

I was dripping wet again and had to change into my last dry clothes behind some trees before we started again.

"If we find a dryer, or a clothes line, we need to stop," I said. Ryan laughed, obviously pleased I was back to being almost normal.

But I wasn't normal. The river had changed me. The earthquake, the tidal wave, even those robbers. That had been terrifying, but not final like the river. I had known I would die. I'd almost accepted it only to be pulled back from certain death by Ryan.

A thing like that changes a girl. Changes her in ways she can't even know.

Chapter Nine

Ryan

My gut refused to unclench. The sight of Kelsey being pulled under the water would haunt me for years.

Glancing over at her, I had to shake my head. She'd bounced back fast. You would never know that an hour earlier she'd almost died. That thought made me readjust my thinking about Kelsey Morgan. She had a lot more steel than I would ever have imagined.

What else had I been wrong about? I mean I'd thought of her as the air head cheerleader type. You know, more concerned about being popular. Wow, how wrong could a person be? There was so much more depth to her.

Those thoughts led me to thinking about when we got to Spokane. I'd end up leaving her with her mom and head up to my Papa's and then go find my sister. And things had changed. Two hundred miles distance was the same as being across the continent before the railroad. A person wasn't going to just drop by for the day.

Shaking off the thought, I focused on putting one foot in front of the other. The pack straps bit into my shoulders and my legs felt like rubber. Constantly walking uphill was getting old. At least it wasn't raining. Barely.

The gray clouds were brushing against the top of the mountains and threatened to open up again on a whim.

Most of the storm had left us and was dumping rain on the Rockies by now. But I had the feeling we were in for another wave. If it had been winter or we were higher we'd be snowed in under sixteen feet of powder. What else would go wrong I wondered as my stomach clenched up tight? I was responsible for getting these people back to their families. It puts a burden on a guy. Was this what Dad felt all the time? The pressure to think about stuff going bad before it did?

"Hey," Tania yelled from the side of a car as she reached in and pulled out a pink puffy coat. Smiling from ear to ear she dropped her pack then her light jacket and pulled it on. "A perfect fit," she yelled as she twisted, modeling it for us.

I laughed, the kids were doing good. The storm hadn't changed them. They'd crossed that river. I was lucky. They weren't whiners or too terrified to even move. I thought about some people I knew and shuddered. It could have been so much worse.

Two hours into our walk and Kelsey fell in next to me. I mean I sort of preferred it when she was in front. I liked watching those jean-clad hips swish back and forth. Of course, I'd never say that so I wisely kept my mouth shut.

"There is a ton of houses up at the summit, rentals," she said. "Mom and I stayed in one last year to go skiing. What do you think?"

"I bet they are full of people from the road," I replied. "But we'll see."

She frowned for a moment, shooting me weird looks from beneath her brow. What did she want me to say? Things will be great. We'll find a nice house, fully stocked with food. Come on. No way.

She glanced at me again then hurried forward to talk to Julia. I just shrugged. I swear, I will never learn how to just talk to people. She asked a question, I answered with what I thought.

The last bit before the summit was tiring but we were almost there. We started seeing houses, some with candles or lamps in the window. A gas station with empty shelves. Dead ski lifts over barren slopes. The occasional person darting into a small cabin. Like I thought, I think every one was occupied

Reaching over, I attached Jake's leash and yelled for everyone to bunch up.

"I think the Inn," Kelsey said pointing to a long building on the other side of a huge parking lot. "They might have a room. They've got a restaurant."

Shrugging, I adjusted my pack and made my pistol more comfortable in my waistband then pulled my coat closed to cover it. I knew the rules had changed but I wasn't sure everyone else was thinking the same way.

We crossed the empty parking lot. I had to smile. Last winter this would have been full with people coming up to hit the ski slopes. Thousands of people. Some staying overnight in rentals or the Inn. Others just up for the day.

The last of the snow had been washed away by the storm.

Paul held the door as we stepped into the main office. A storm lantern flickering light across the room. An older man, maybe in his fifties, heavyset with a bald head greeted us. "Welcome," he said smiling at us like we were his long-lost children.

I was about to ask for a room when a small mountain of a man stepped in from the back, an AR-15 semi-auto strapped to his shoulder. A large red beard. Flannel shirt. My gut clenched when I saw his eyes. This guy knew the new rules. That was definite.

The heavyset guy smiled at the small mountain and patted him on the shoulder. He saw our concern and said, "Don't worry about Turner." He then turned to us and pulled out an old green ledger book that looked older than Noah's Ark.

"The cell towers and computers are down. Have been for two days. Just leave your credit card and we'll charge it when they're back up."

My jaw dropped as I stared at the man. "Um …" I was at a loss for words. Didn't these people know what was going on? I mean there were a hundred cars abandoned on the highway. This wasn't a power outage.

"Um, Things aren't coming back."

Both men frowned at me. "What do you mean? When the government gets this stuff fixed we'll just run your credit card charge both your room and meals."

The kids looked at me. I could see the doubt in their eyes. Here was an adult. They couldn't be this wrong.

"There is no government. Everything from Issaquah to the ocean is gone."

The color drained from the man's face.

"We just came from Seattle. We saw it. Everything not destroyed by the earthquake was wiped off the face of the earth by the tidal wave. The Asteroid caused an EMP. The power is not coming back on. Even if they could fix it. They can't move the equipment to where it's needed."

Both men looked at each other then back at us. I could see it in their eyes. Who was this kid?

"He's right," Kelsey said. "That's why the cars don't work. Even if you had power the computers won't ever work again. No one is coming to help."

They stared at us for a long moment, the heavyset man's brow knitted. "You came from Seattle? You're the first from that direction."

I nodded, "I imagine most walked down to North Bend. More civilization."

He stared off into nothing for a long moment then turned to the guy with the rifle. "We've only had people stuck locally. Within five miles or so. Where did everyone else go? And have you seen any linemen working? I mean, I haven't even seen a state trooper."

Had these people really been this obtuse? Or had they just been so used to things being solved for them they couldn't fathom it all being gone.

Finally, the heavyset guy said, "Um. You lot go into the restaurant. It's on me. I need to get people together they need to hear this."

I was about to argue then saw the look in Paul's eyes. Food. A man never turns down free food. "Um. Thanks," I said then motioned for my group to go through the door on the right towards the restaurant. I guessed we'd work out the room details later.

The smell of hot food made my stomach grumble. The restaurant looked like any pancake house you've ever seen. Booth and tables. A few people hunched over their food. The counter had been set up with a steam table. A lady in a hair net stood behind it waiting for us.

I couldn't not smile. Who was going to enforce the OSHA hygiene laws now?

"We've got biscuits with and without gravy," she said with a coarse voice.

I laughed as I motioned for the others to grab some paper plates.

"We've got to use it up before it spoils," she said as she put two biscuits on each plate and covered them in big scoops of pan gravy with chunks of ground beef.

They must be using propane for cooking, I thought as I led the others to a table in the middle. We dropped our packs and shoveled in our food. I was scraping the last speck off my plate when the back door opened and people started coming in. Couples, and families. A guy who looked like he drove a truck. Just people. The men looked like they hadn't shaved in days. The women looked harried and nervous.

I imagined most of the other people on the road had taken up the empty rental houses. Only the leftovers had ended up here in the Inn.

Heavyset guy followed them in. Maybe two dozen or so. Mountain Man behind him. Then two more armed men. One a young guy with a scraggly goutte the other a forty-year-old with thin blond hair. Both men had rifles slung over their shoulders and pistols on their hips.

My gut tightened. Why all the firepower?

The heavyset guy raised his hands to get everyone's attention. "For those who haven't met me. I'm Bill Pearson, manager of the Snoqualmie Inn." He smiled at each person. The man knows how to work a room I thought. He had everyone's attention.

His smile dropped to be replaced by a serious frown. "Unfortunately. We've just learned that Seattle might be damaged."

I scoffed and stood up. "It's not damaged, it's gone. Everything from the foothills to the ocean is gone from Vancouver to San Diego."

People froze, staring at me bug-eyed like I'd just denied the moon landing or that the earth wasn't round. But I ignored them and indicated Kelsey. "We saw it happen. We were the last ones out. Ten minutes slower and we'd be dead."

At first, there was only silence then suddenly a thousand questions. The truck driver cursed and called my mother a bad name then said he wasn't listening to some dumb kid.

I glared at them, "The asteroid set off an earthquake, a tidal wave, and an EMP. That's why your cars don't work."

Still, people looked doubtful until a man in a suit but no tie said, "The kid is right. It had to be an EMP. And if the asteroid CNN was talking about actually hit us. Then it'd do that kind of damage."

"I did see a bright flash just before the car stopped," An older lady said with a shake of her head.

"What about Everett," A mother with two children asked with fear in her eyes.

"Gone," I said as my heart fell.

Both children began to cry, the youngest asking about their father. The woman looked as if I'd just pronounced her death sentence. She wrapped her arms around the two crying children and pulled them into a hug.

People started talking to each other, bouncing off theories and questions. I let them begin to work it out then told them the hard truth. "No one is coming to help. Even if they wanted to, no vehicle is moving. Ever again."

The rumble of talk slammed to a halt. Panic, I could see it in their eyes. The truth was hitting them. They were stuck far from home. Far from their people. The future was unknown and they weren't ready. Yes, they were seconds from full-blown panic.

Kelsey reached over and took my hand, squeezing it, showing them that she stood with me, agreed with what I was saying. We stood there and let them come to grips with this new reality. It was strange. Some looked at us thankful for the news, Others shot us pure hate for telling them their world was ruined.

What had these people been doing for three days? How could they be this out of touch? But then I began to realize. Of course they were out of touch. There was no news. No contact with anyone from the outside. Besides, the people who had figured it out had been the ones to head for North Bend and civilization. Only the people with their heads stuck in the sand had stayed where they were.

Bill Pearson raised his hands again and called, "People, people, We need to figure this out."

Still, they mumbled and grumbled amongst themselves then the trucker guy asked, "What about our rooms."

Bill smiled, "Don't worry about it. No one is going to get kicked out. We've got food."

A silent sigh echoed through the room, one problem eliminated. But then Mr. Mountain Man stepped forward, unslung his rifle from his shoulder, and fired three shots into the ceiling.

I froze. Everyone froze. No one had expected that. They'd been listening. Holding the panic at bay. Now this monstrosity of a man had changed their world once again.

My hand started to inch towards the pistol in my waist but Kelsey pulled it back, "No," she whispered. "You'll get us all killed."

Unfortunately, she was right so I let my hand drop to my side.

Mr. Mountain Man stepped forward and said, "There is new management. Everyone has to leave." The gleam in his eye let me know how much he was enjoying this.

"What?"

"Huh?

"Bill?"

Bill Pearson turned on his employee with a heavy frown. "Don't be ridiculous. Of course they can stay."

Mountain Man scoffed. "You said it yourself. Ain't no state troopers. You're letting these people eat our food. We should be saving it."

My stomach clenched. This wasn't going to end well. The straggly goutte guy giggled.

"I'm still in charge here," Bill growled as he reached for the man's rifle.

Mountain Man laughed, lowered his weapon, and shot Bill through the chest. I gulped as I pushed my crowd to the floor. Unable to believe what I had just seen. Mr. Mountain Man had murdered a man in front of twenty witnesses like he'd stepped on a cockroach.

People screamed and scrambled. Turning my head, I looked, Bill's sightless eyes stared back at me as blood spilled out from beneath him.

"Okay, people," Mountain Man called out. "You can leave or you can die. I don't care which. And ain't anyone ever going to say we can't."

Every part of my soul wanted to kill this man. If any man deserved it this man did. But my responsibility was to keep my people alive. It took every bit of control but I was able to pull my hate and anger back under control and slowly pushed up off the ground.

I held my breath waiting to be shot.

Mountain Man just nodded for the door. "Get out. Everyone. Not back to your rooms. Just out. I see anyone in this building ten seconds from now, I start shooting."

"What about our stuff," suite man asked.

Mountain Man smiled, "It's ours now. Out."

I started pulling my people up off the ground. One thing I knew for sure, this man was not going to give us a second chance. When I helped Kelsey up I noticed scraggly goutte guy point to her and whisper something to the mountain man.

The big guy looked at Kelsey then shook his head as he said something that disappointed goutte guy.

"Go," I said as I reached down for my pack.

"Leave it," the big guy yelled as he leveled his rifle right at me, daring me to move one more inch toward my pack. I froze. We needed our stuff to survive. Then I saw the look in Goutte guy's eyes as he stared at Kelsey and knew I had to get her out of there.

Abandoning my pack, I started pushing her and the others to the door. She hesitated. "Just go," I growled. Most of the others were still on the ground, too stunned to react.

"Five Seconds," Mountain Man yelled as we pushed through the door. Once outside I kept them going. The look in Scraggly Goutte's eyes told me I had to get Kelsey out of there.

"Our stuff," Paul said.

"Just go, go, east. We need to get away from here."

The shock in their eyes told me just how much they had been impacted. I imagine they had never been touched by death. Their teacher had disappeared under that hill of rocks. The asteroid had been so distant. This was but a few feet away. The visual would haunt their nightmares for years.

We were maybe a hundred feet away when I turned back to look and saw goutte guy step out, his head twisting back and forth, looking for his prey.

"Run," I yelled as I pushed them towards the highway. Kelsey looked where I had looked and gulped as the color drained from her face. She had seen it too. She was a pretty girl, she knew that look and now knew there was nothing to stop an animal.

We began to run. Jake barked, asking why but willing to enjoy the fun. I kept looking over my shoulder, terrified the man would start firing, determined that if he couldn't have her then no one could.

But he didn't fire, he just started running after us.

"Keep going," I said as I pulled my pistol and started to fall back, letting them get a dozen feet in front. Kelsey suddenly saw what I was doing and came back pulling at my arm.

I was going to pull away but I saw we were putting distance between us and our pursuer so I kept up with them. We hit the main highway and started positioning cars and trucks between us and the man chasing us.

Fortunately, we wanted to live more than he wanted Kelsey. I'm sure a hundred yards into the chase he began to realize there were easier targets and fell off. Either that or he was a druggy and had the lungs of a bashful mouse.

I kept them going until we got a mile down the road then Julia started to whimper, holding her side.

"We can walk now," I said as I shot another look over my shoulder.

We bent at the waist and gulped in air. Finally, Kelsey straightened up and said, "What just happened?"

"I don't know," I said to her. "But we need to keep going. If they change their minds, I want to be so far away it isn't worth the effort."

She looked back at me then nodded before saying. "What now? You can't say it's still fifty, fifty."

I laughed, "Maybe ten percent chance."

She stared back at me, "That good? I would have said five."

Chapter Ten

Kelsey

Would it ever end? The constant gut gnawing worry. Every moment seemed filled with dread and danger. Would we ever feel safe again? I still couldn't get the sight of Bill Pearsons lying in a puddle of blood out of my mind. It was so final. So unnecessary.

And Ryan. I had seen it in his eyes, the need to fight back against men with rifles. But I'd also seen him go out of his way to place himself between our pursuer and the rest of us. Hanging back, willing to be shot so we could survive.

My heart ached thinking about what he had done. It was obvious what that weirdo had wanted. If Ryan hadn't acted so quickly I might have been taken to a back room and used by three different men. The thought sent a cold shiver down my spine.

Instead, I was free. Yes, without our stuff. But alive.

"We need to be checking cars," Ryan said. "Blankets, food, water bottles, even empty ones. Anything."

The kids nodded. I could see the absent stares. As if they had checked out. Their minds refusing to deal with what they had seen and done. Silent tears dripped down Julia's cheeks. Her brother Paul kept glancing over his shoulder obviously terrified at what might come.

Ryan took a deep breath then said, "We're not dead. There is a way out of this. You people get your heads on straight and we'll make it."

They stared back at him dead-eyed, unable to process his words. "Jesus guys, snap out of it. Paul. You go with Kelsey to the other side to check the cars. Julia, take Jake. Tania find me a big rock. Something I can use to break windows if necessary.

Giving them tasks seemed to break them out of it and we started working as a team again. But my insides continued to churn. We had escaped one terror. But what about the future? My life looked like it would be filled with constant fear.

"And keep moving," Ryan yelled at us across the median.

I nodded back before peaking into the first car. Nothing of course. We fell into a routine. While one checked out a car the other would continue to the next. We found a full bottle of water in one. A pack of gum in another. Then the jackpot, a large quilt in the back of a Cadillac. A multi-colored flower theme. It looked like something a grandmother would make and she was delivering it to her grandkids.

Paul and I sort of struck out after that then went through a long stretch of no cars followed by more empties. I could only shake my head. People traveled so lightly. Never worrying about being stuck somewhere. There was always civilization around, they would always be safe.

Every time I glanced over at Ryan I would feel a twinge of worry. They didn't look like they were having any success. Then Ryan yelled and pointed. A Safeway semi. Obviously delivering groceries to the supermarket to the west.

I yelled and pulled Paul to join them, my heart racing with anticipation.

Ryan smiled as he waited for us to join them. Once we were all gathered at the back of the truck he raised his large rock and brought it down on the padlock. It bounced but didn't break. He grumbled under his breath then hit the lock even harder.

It snapped open. Ryan smiled at me then removed the remains of the lock and opened the back. We held our breath then moaned with sadness. Empty. The entire truck was empty.

"No," Paul cursed.

Ryan laughed and shook his head. "We should have known it wouldn't be that easy."

Suddenly his eyes grew big as he pointed behind us.

My stomach clenched as I turned to see another storm coming in. Without thinking I rolled my eyes. Julia gasped. Tanya cursed.

"We need to find a car," Ryan said. "Something unlocked. I don't want to have to break a window to get in."

The kids glanced back at the approaching storm then started to race down the road. The wind had shifted sending a coldness over us.

"Here," Paul called as he opened the back door to a Ford Pickup. The kids hurried into the back just as the rain started to swish down the road towards us. I jumped into the front and slid over to make room for Ryan. I swear he slammed the door shut just as we were swallowed by the storm.

I checked out our home for the night. A bench seat up front and in back. Roomy. The light had faded as the rain pounded so loudly it hurt my ears.

"Spread out the quilt," I yelled over the rain as I looked in the back. Jake was down on the floorboard, looking up at me with expectant eyes as his tail bounced twice.

Paul spread it over the three of them and I sighed internally, they'd be warm enough.

"Now what?" I asked Ryan.

He clenched his jaw then looked back west where we had come from. I could see it in his eyes, he was thinking about going back.

"No," I said to him with my fiercest stare. "You are not going to try and get our stuff back."

He looked at me like I didn't understand. "In the storm, I could get in close. They'd never hear me or see me."

"Maybe," I said. "or they could kill you for trying, and then who would save us? Who would save your sister?"

I could see that I'd hit my target when he winced. I hated fighting dirty. But I didn't have a choice here. We needed Ryan. Spokane was too far away and too much was going to go wrong between here and there.

His face slowly shifted from pain to determination and I knew I was going to lose him and suddenly I realized just how much that would hurt. I knew if he went back he'd be killed and I wouldn't only lose a possible savior. I would lose someone I cared about. Someone who had become dear to me.

"Ryan," I said as I reached over and took his hand in mine. "Please. You can't risk it."

He continued to waver then I asked, "What percentage if we don't? What do we drop down to? One percent?" But I could see the resignation in his eyes.

Like I said I don't mind fighting dirty when I have to.

He sighed then nodded before turning to stare out at the storm. I think I knew what going on in his mind. That male ego thing. He felt like a failure. In his mind, he'd been defeated. In my mind, I thought he had won by getting us away. But I'm not a guy and don't understand how they see the world.

I was about to tell him my thoughts when I forced myself to shut up. I had won our argument. Talking about it would only risk him changing his mind. Just shut u[Kelsey I had to tell myself a dozen times while I waited for him to accept it.

Still, the storm raged, the wind rocking the truck, the rain pounding into the metal like a snare drum. The light slowly began to fade. I glanced in the back. The three kids were huddled together under the quilt, Julia in the middle. They would be alright I assured myself then shivered as the temperature continued to fall.

Would it snow? God, No! we would surely die. Please, I prayed. Don't let it snow.

Ryan glanced over and saw me shiver then reached over his back to take off his coat.

"No," I said, "you'll freeze. I'm not taking your coat."

His brow knotted for a moment then he removed it anyway and said, "We'll share. Come here."

I hesitated for a moment as my heart bounced around for a moment then I took a deep breath. He was right. We needed to share body warmth.

Biting down on my back teeth, I slid across the seat to sit next to him. He laughed then put his coat over the both of us and pulled me close.

Okay, new knowledge. A boy's arms. The right boy's arms, can make a girl feel safe and secure. I feeling of rightness filled me as he held me. I felt myself sink into him as I rested my head in the crook of his shoulder.

YES. I thought as I sighed and let myself just be. Let myself relax.

His grip tightened just a bit as if he understood and was letting me know it was okay. Like I said, the perfect feeling of security.

Don't forget, I had grown up without a dad. The boys I had known in school had been more handsy than huggy. If you know what I mean. So I wasn't used to this feeling.

Ryan leaned down and said, "You were right. About not going back for our stuff. Just don't get used to it. Winning an argument."

I laughed and snuggled in closer. Oh, if he only knew how much I had won. I kept him safe to hold me and keep the horrors of the world at bay. I had won so much he would never understand.

And still, the storm rocked the truck.

As I lay there I fought to get the memory of what had happened only hours earlier out of my mind. We really had lost everything. And those people, the ones staying in the Inn? What happened to them? Had they gotten out in time? Had that big man really started shooting them? I hadn't heard shots. But I had been running, scared out of my mind. Who knew what happened?

Get used to it, I told myself. This gut-wrenching fear. Get used to it.

I lay in Ryan's arms and thought about the boy holding me. I had been so lucky in so many ways. Yes, my world was ruined but I was alive because of him. But there was more. I could trust him I realized. I mean on so many levels. I just knew he was like a rock in a raging river. Literally, I thought with a smile.

But there was something deep inside that wondered about him and what he wanted. I mean I was used to guys always hitting on me. Sometimes it seemed that was my only interaction with the males of the species. That constant pushing for more. Those subtle and not-so-subtle hints and sometimes outright requests for intimacy.

But not Ryan. He wasn't like that. He didn't flirt. Didn't suggest. Didn't smile at me with a hidden agenda. A part of me was almost hurt but mostly confused. Why? Was it me? And yes, I knew the world had ended and the boy might have other things on his mind. But still, it made a girl wonder.

I mean even now. It was dark and I was wrapped up in his arms. But I didn't have to worry about his hand drifting to where it shouldn't. It was just unusual, I'm saying. This feeling of not worrying. Not having to be on guard.

Deciding to just not think about it I let myself relax and closed my eyes.

I woke with a start. Warm, Ryan still holding me as I fought to understand what had pulled me out of my sleep.

The rain had stopped, I realized. The wind had ceased roaring. Another night survived, I said to myself as I again relaxed and returned to dreaming about a tall boy with brown hair using a sword against a mountain troll.

The next time I woke the sun was peaking beneath the clouds as it came up between two mountain peaks. Ryan squeezed my shoulder and I knew he was already awake. How long? I wondered suddenly terrified he had been watching me sleep. Watching me drool all over myself.

As if reading my mind he scoffed then indicated I should get up off of him. Of course, I realized, the boy was probably tired of a clinging girl soaking up all his warmth and energy.

He shot me a quick smile then opened the door and stepped outside before opening the back door and tapping his leg for Jake. The two of them disappeared into the forest for a few minutes. I was able to breathe when they came back out.

After our morning routine, the six of us started down the road. Ryan passed out a stick of gum each for our breakfast. My heart fell as my mouth watered. I needed more food. I mean it had been a rather hectic few days to say the least. We'd climbed mountains, ran for our lives. And been hit with a dozen terrifying emotions.

My stomach tightened, demanding to be fed.

Glancing over at the others I could see it in their eyes. They were hungry and it was going to get worse. We shared the one bottle of water then Ryan pointed at a stream of water racing down the road from last night's rain. "We won't die of thirst."

As we descended the mountains we continued to check every vehicle. We found a wool blanket and my heart sort of hitched, did this mean I wouldn't get to rest in Ryan's arms? We also found three cigarette lighters, and a romance novel that Ryan insisted we take.

"For starting fires," he answered to my questioning look.

But no food.

It was mid-day and Ryan called a halt. We sat on a log under the trees. Paul laughed, "I never thought I would miss my pack."

We all laughed and I felt things shift between us. The nightmares from yesterday were being put aside. We had to focus on surviving.

Ryan said, "We should hit a town soon. I think it is Easton. Then there are others. We will find something."

I looked back at him. We'd found civilization in North Bend, looted a store then almost been robbed. We'd found civilization in the Inn and almost been killed. Hadn't he been the one to say we should be invisible?

He read my thoughts and shrugged. "We don't have a choice."

My stomach turned over that we would once again have to voluntarily go into the jaws of the beast and risk everything if we were to find what we needed to survive.

The question was. Which would kill us first, the lack of supplies or the quest to get said supplies?

Chapter Twelve

Ryan

Easton was a small village lining the highway. Gas stations, a Motel 6. A few houses. The gas stations were empty, picked clean. I could imagine a horde of people descending on them and stripping everything like a cloud of locusts.

The cafés were closed. One had its windows broken. Again, I was pretty sure it had been picked clean.

"Wow," Kelsey said when we found the third café burned to the ground. I could see it in her eyes as she twisted to look around. Several businesses had broken windows.

"What do we do?" Julia asked with a touch of panic in her voice.

I shrugged, "We keep moving."

My heart hurt, It was well past lunch time. It'd soon be twenty-four hours since our last meal. What happened when that stretched into forty-eight, or seventy-two, or a hundred forty-four?

The few people we saw shot us angry stares, obviously worried we would try to take what they had found.

When we got out of town Paul fell back to walk with me. "What are we going to do?" he asked. Man to man.

I was tempted to ask him. To put the guilt and responsibility on his shoulders. That was how far I had come, I was going to unload everything onto a thirteen-year-old boy and just walk away. But thankfully, I hadn't sunk that low. "We'll figure it out."

He shot me a doubtful stare from beneath his brow then sighed heavily, obviously upset at me.

"Keep checking cars," I said to him and sent him and Kelsey to the other side.

But it soon became evident that we were tail-end Charlies. Other people had been there before us. Car windows were broken, doors left open. A cold fear began to eat at my gut. If it was like this we were in a world of hurt.

When we got to Cle Elum, Kelsey pointed to a Safeway sign and raised an eyebrow. I shrugged. It wouldn't hurt to check it out. Unfortunately, when we got there we found a line of people and two county sheriffs outside.

"What's the deal?" I asked the last person in line.

He shot me a concerned look then told me, "One plastic bag per family per day. It's free but you only get one. If they find you taking more they confiscate it all from you and ban you from coming back."

I made my people get in line as my heart jumped. Kelsey's stomach rumbled. She shot me a look of happiness. We were going to get food.

"I want steak," Paul said. "You can get a lot of steak in a bag."

Tania rolled her eyes but didn't come outright and call him stupid. I just clenched my jaw as I tried to figure out what would provide the most calories.

When our turn came I was hoping they'd give us each a bag but the sheriff just scoffed and said, one per family as he handed me a flashlight. I gave Paul our rolled-up blankets.

The others fell out as I took the bag into the store and felt my heart drop. The shelves were bare. So much for steak. Or rice, or flour, or anything in bulk. I'd be lucky to find a jar of olives and I hated olives.

Two other people were snaking their way through the aisles. I started on the far end. Somethings hadn't been touched, Pickled eggs, powdered curry sauce, capers. But I did find a box of white cake mix on the back of a top shelf. Some times there is a benefit for being tall. I also found six cans of sardines. A jar of sugar-free strawberry jelly, and best of all, a box of ritz crackers sitting forlornly all alone in the middle of the shelf.

A sense of hope filled me. We could stretch this stuff for two days if we had to. I looked down at my bag and saw I still had some room so I stopped in the fruit aisle and picked up enough apples to make the bag bulge and threaten to break.

When I got outside I handed the cop the flashlight then shot my people a quick smile.

Kelsey peaked inside the bag then gave me a questioning look.

"Hey, I got what I could. There won't be any tomorrow."

She nodded her understanding then pointed across the parking lot at a hardware store.

"I bet they're not giving away camping gear," I said. She gave me a look and shook her head, obviously upset at my negativity.

But unfortunately, I was proven right. Three big mem stood outside, each cradling a twelve gauge shotgun in their arms.

"We ain't taking cash," the older man said. "No credit cards. Just trade."

I sighed inside as I thought about those gold chains I had bought in North Bend. Kelsey looked over at me with regret and I knew she was thinking the same thing.

"How about this," Julia said as she reached into her shirt and pulled out a silver cross on a silver chain.

"No," Paul said, "That was Grandma's."

Julia glared at him and said, "She wouldn't want us dying. Sort of goes against the grandma code."

I laughed. It seemed Julia was getting tougher each day.

The old man bent forward to examine the jewelry then nodded. "I'll let you have twenty dollars worth."

"Thirty," I said.

He frowned, in a fake upset look, but I was pretty sure he was enjoying bargaining. Besides he knew we were desperate. "Twenty-Five."

"Done," I said, "And no taxes."

He laughed then motioned for his men to let me in. Julia took off her necklace, kissed the cross goodbye then handed it to him.

I gave Kelsey the bag of food and went inside, pleased to see that they'd set up Coleman lanterns that gave off enough light to see where a person was going.

Survival stuff, I told myself. I immediately headed for the sportsman section and whooped. Enough fishing tackle to outfit half of Seattle. I grabbed a spool of twenty-pound test, a packet of hooks, and another of split weights. Twelve dollars I realized as I totaled it in my head.

What else did we need?

Everything, I realized but ended up getting a cheap tarp and realized I had three dollars left. I spent the next twenty minutes searching for the perfect thing to make up that last three dollars. Desperate to not waste it. Finally, I found a pot and a spoon.

The beginnings of a new life, I thought to myself, surprised at how happy I was at having even these meager things.

When I stepped out of the store the older man handed his shotgun to his partner then went through my stuff. "Twenty-Seven Forty-Eight,"

I gulped. "Come on man."

He frowned then finally shrugged accepting my deal. Wow, the sense of elation shooting through me was a surprise.

I got them out of town and divided a sleeve of ritz crackers, five each and one can of sardines. Jake was given crackers but I held the sardines for us. It was just enough food to remind us how hungry we were but it took the edge off.

We continued down the road and when it started to get dark I found us an SUV that hadn't had its windows smashed. The night was long and lonely. Bench seats I told myself. Next time find bench seats, I missed holding Kelsey in my arms.

I broke out two sleeves of crackers and the jar of jelly. Again it wasn't enough but it was better than nothing.

The next day we passed through Ellensburg. I glanced over at the college and shook my head. Eight months from now I was supposed to be attending classes there. God, I had so looked forward to college. A chance to start a new life. Meet new people, and learn new stuff. The beginning that would now never happen.

Kelsey caught me looking and gave me a sad smile. She knew what was going through my mind. That was another surprise. Who could have ever imagined Kelsey Morgan would know me well enough to read my mind?

Unfortunately, Ellensburg wasn't set up to help strangers. They'd been hit with enough outsiders. College kids, tourists in town when the asteroid hit. Their food wasn't going to last long. And the farms in the area wouldn't harvest their crops for another five months.

Cops and helpers were stationed along the highway to make sure we kept moving and didn't drop down off the highway into their town.

We pushed through town and came down off the mountains onto the dry foothills of eastern Washington. Only they weren't so dry anymore. More a morass of mud that I knew would get worse as we hit the flatlands.

We spent the nights in cars. I cooked up the cake mix and the last of the jelly. We ate off of it all day. But we were out of food again.

We kept pushing on and finally came to the Bridge over the Columbia at Vantage Lake. the water was high, lapping at the bridge, reminding me of the river crossing up in the mountains. But we got across without a problem.

That late afternoon, seven days into our trip we couldn't find a car that hadn't been destroyed. It seemed someone had come through and used a baseball bat on every window. Kids, I thought as I clenched my teeth, taking out their fear and anger.

"That's okay," I said as I pointed to a swollen muddy pond off to the side with a large cedar tree standing sentinel. "We'll use the tarp for a tent. It'll give me time to set some snares, go fishing."

They stared back at me and my insides tightened into a hard ball. Their cheeks were getting gaunt, their eyes had that sunken-in appearance. And It had only been a few days. What would they look like a few weeks from now?

I had to use fishing line quadrupled up between the cedar tree and a small pine maybe four feet off the ground. I draped the tarp over, used my buck knife to carve some stakes, and pounded them into the grommets with a heavy rock.

"Wow, we are back in the stone age," Paul said as he held the other side of the tarp.

I laughed, the kid wasn't far wrong. While they gathered firewood I rigged up a hand line and headed for the pond. Please I begged. We needed food. I caught a couple of grasshoppers and used them as bait.

Within minutes, I had a dozen perch and one small trout. Then just as they had started biting they stopped. Well, they'd get us through the night. We filleted the fish getting a dozen small chunks of meat. Once they were devoured I used the fish carcasses to cook up a fish stew.

Again, it was just enough to keep us going. But it beat the alternative.

Kelsey smiled and said, "Thank you for dinner."

Tania picked the last shred of fish off a bone then said, "It's weird, I don't think I've ever tasted anything so good. I mean, my dad took me to a special restaurant. And the food was good. They had this fiery dessert that was unbelievable. But it doesn't come close to a scrawny fish on the side of the road.

Everyone laughed, agreeing.

We kept the fire going, enjoying a moment of relaxation. No one talked, obviously too afraid to disturb the peace. But eventually, Julia yawned. I told them it was time for bed. That was the thing about no food. Nobody had any energy.

I busied myself putting out the fire then realized they'd left a spot on the end for me next to Kelsey. Had that been her idea? Okay, I'll admit, the idea of sleeping next to a beautiful girl was sort of cool. But it was going to be hard keeping my hands to myself.

That was one thing I knew for sure. Kelsey Morgan didn't want me hitting on her like every other guy in her life. Especially not just after the world ended.

I slithered in under the tarp and turned my back to Kelsey. She flopped the blanket over me then pulled her hands in under her head. I glanced over my shoulder and saw in the dying light that she was staring at me.

"What?" I asked.

She gave me a strange look then turned over away from me. What was that all about, I wondered as I fought the urge to pull her into my embrace. Yes, it was going to be a long hard night.

Chapter Eleven

Kelsey

I woke with the delicious feeling of Ryan wrapped around me. His legs in behind my knees, his arms draped over me, his hand on my stomach holding me tight. The smell of woodsmoke and leather enveloped me. I closed my eyes and soaked up the feeling of rightness.

But the morning came. A dull gray morning. What would happen today I wondered as my stomach grumbled. God, would I ever feel full again? I had been on small diets in my life. Nothing serious. A few pounds I needed to lose before the cheer season started. But this wasn't a diet. I couldn't cheat. I couldn't ignore it and adjust my goals. This was too real.

I was hungry. A stomach-gnawing hunger that made a person look at the world differently. Every thought seemed to revolve around food and where I could find more.

Behind me, Ryan took a deep breath and I knew he was awake.

"Morning Princess," he said as he pulled away.

I couldn't help but smile. I liked it when he called me princess. Yes, I knew he had started calling me that as a put-down. But, now, his voice sounded different. Almost as if he believed I was special.

With no breakfast, it didn't take us long to hit the road. My stomach cramped, demanding food. But we were out of luck. Every car had been emptied. The houses along the way looked dangerous. Some would have men outside patrolling the fence line. Others looked empty, doors open to the elements, informing us they'd already been raided.

Twice we saw bodies laying in the front yards. I had no idea if they were the attackers or defenders. But they were people who would not see the next sunrise.

Just as I thought things couldn't get any worse, a cold wind tickled the back of my neck. I turned and cursed. "Not again."

Ryan looked back and sighed. Another heavy bank of dark clouds was approaching. As we watched a lightning bolt shot from cloud to cloud. We both started scanning for a place to hide but the road was empty.

"Run," Ryan yelled as he started to jog east then cranked it up to full sprint. The wind behind us grew stronger, plucking at our clothes as the six of us raced down the road.

"There," he yelled and pointed to a semi-truck stopped in the middle of the road on the other side. We rushed across the median just as the rain hit. Big fat raindrops that hurt. No hail, I realized as my heart jumped. Hail, not sleet. I could survive rain. But not a thousand ice pellets.

"Under the trailer," Ryan yelled over the wind then stood as a wind brake as we each scrambled under the trailer. The wind howled and the ice pinged off the trailer and the road.

We scrunched together. Ryan wrapped his arm over us trying to protect us. I just buried my head in the back of Tania and held on, praying for it all to stop.

The hail continued. Lightening flashed and thunder rolled over us. But we were safe, I tried to convince myself. Starving, hiding under a trailer. But we would survive. At least for today.

The storm seemed to go on for half of forever but eventually, it began to back off and shifted over to just rain followed by a drizzle then nothing.

We continued to cower under the trailer until Ryan pulled his arm back and slid out from beneath the truck.

"It's clear," He said then helped us out.

"How much longer?" I asked. "What else is going to go wrong?"

Ryan shrugged his shoulders and I swear I saw a hint of guilt in his eyes. It was eating him up that he couldn't provide what we needed. My heart hurt. I had made things harder for him by complaining. And there was nothing I could do to ease his burden.

If I told him it was okay, he'd know I was lying. Thankfully, Julia saw it too and simply patted his shoulder and gave him a quick smile. The look of hero worship in her eyes told me just how much she cared for him.

What surprised me was the sudden jealous feeling that flashed through me. I know, ridiculous. If you had told me a week ago that I'd feel angry about some thirteen-year-old girl touching Ryan Conrad I would have called you crazy as a bat.

But now, I had to take a deep breath to try and stop myself from reaching out and slapping her hand away from him.

Ryan was oblivious, of course, thankfully, like most boys, he didn't pick up on the signals girls sent them.

We continued on, The next town was gone, burnt to the ground. Nothing but blackened timbers mixed with gray ash washed together with the local mud. "What happened?" I asked with shock.

Ryan shook his head. "No fire department. No trucks. No pumps. Probably happened the first day. A gas line broke in the earthquake. Fire started, no way to put it out. It spread and burnt them out."

My God. They'd lost everything. And yes, I knew how they must have felt.

"Where'd the people go?" Paul asked.

139

"Family, friends, local farms, the road," Ryan said as he kicked a charred timber out of our way. "Doesn't matter," he continued. "Not our problem."

I shot him a surprised look. Had he always been this callus? No, I realized. But the fight for survival made a person focus on the main problem, staying alive.

We pushed through the town, silent, each lost in our own thoughts. Two miles later Julia shifted to walk next to Ryan. And yes, my alarms went to full alert as I fell back to join them. She shot me a quick frown but I noticed she didn't try flirting with him.

I really couldn't blame her, I realized. I mean, she was young, on the cusp of womanhood, the world had just ended. So of course, she wanted to attach herself to the biggest, strongest male around.

But no, that wasn't going to happen.

Paul suddenly called out and pointed, a single column of smoke was rising from a farmhouse about two miles off the road.

I quickly glanced at the fields between the road and the house and felt my heart fall. The storms had turned them into muddy quagmires. Between four feet of rain and a ton of hail, The crops had been flattened and would never ripen.

"Maybe they'll trade food for work," I said with more hope than I felt.

Ryan nodded. "Won't hurt to check."

We turned off onto a side road and started for the house. Twice we had to wade through knee-deep water where the road dipped but we eventually came to a wooden gate. Ryan hesitated as he studied the house.

I understood his worry. This wasn't like before. People weren't trusting, the memory of Bill Pearson laying in his blood reminded me what happened to people who trusted others.

"You guys stay here," Ryan said as he unlatched the gate.

"No," I said as I moved to follow him. "They're more likely to feed us if they see girls."

He laughed and shook his head. "They're more likely to kill me and take you and the others."

My heart fell when I realized he was right and stopped from following him.

Ryan slowly approached the house, keeping his hands away from his body. "Hello," he yelled. We stood at the fence holding our breath. So many things could go wrong. Ryan could be shot. They could refuse us food. My insides sank with grief as I realized just how desperate we had become.

He called out twice more from the center of the yard. Finally, the door cracked just a little as the barrel of a rifle peeked through. I gasped expecting a shot. Ryan froze then said, "We just want to talk, maybe work for food."

There was a long silence then an old man stepped out onto the porch, the rifle barrel never waiving.

"Where you from?" the man yelled.

Ryan swallowed then glanced back at us then turned back to the man. "Kelsey and I are from Seattle, headed to Spokane. The others are from Cheney, I'm helping get them home."

The door opened wide as an old grandmother type stepped out to join her husband. "Herman," she said. "They're from Seattle." The hope in her voice made my insides clench up with dread.

"You got out," Herman said. "An army troop passed through two days ago. They said Seattle was gone."

Ryan nodded. "It is, we saw it. We were the last ones out. Everything from Issaquah to the ocean. I imagine it's the same all the way down the coast."

The older woman gasped and held her hand to her throat as the color drained from her face. Her husband gave her a sad look then sighed heavily. "Our daughter, her husband, and the two grandkids lived in Seattle. He worked at Amazon."

My heart sank. Another family destroyed. Dreams, hopes, happiness, all gone forever.

Ryan just nodded. "I'm sorry."

I could tell he really was sorry but he didn't let the matter rest and said, "We haven't eaten in two days. Everything is gone. We were wondering if we could maybe work for a meal."

The man glared at him then out at the destroyed fields. "Won't be any work around here until next spring. And I ain't sure we're going to still be here."

I immediately wondered if he was referring to moving to some new place, or simply dying before next spring.

Ryan nodded then said, "Maybe you've got some wood needs cutting. We can put up a cord or two."

The old man continued to stare at Ryan, obviously fighting himself but his wife gently placed a hand on his shoulder and said, "Herman, if it was our Gracy. We'd want people to help her and the kids."

The old man sighed heavily then dropped his rifle barrel. "There's a load of logs in the back. They need to be split. Was going to do it myself but just don't got the oomph anymore. Doesn't really seem to matter."

Ryan let out a long breath then turned back and smiled and said, "If you've got an axe I can use I'll get to work."

The old man waved his head to the back. Ryan turned and motioned for us to join him.

Our hopes jumped. Maybe we will get some food today.

That was how we spent our afternoon. Paul would place a log on the stump. Ryan would slam the axe into it, splitting it in two. Then repeat. Julia, Tania, and I would stack them on the existing wood pile.

Ten minutes into it, Ryan stopped and pulled his shirt off then returned to splitting logs. I froze as my body reacted. Ryan Conrad was sort of built. Not weirdly gross, but solid. The kind of build that would only grow as he grew older.

There is something about watching a cute guy doing hard physical labor that is just appealing. Subconsciously I licked my lips then caught Julia staring at him with bugged eyes. And nudged her to remind her to start stacking wood.

We worked for two hours until the last log had been split. My stomach continued to clench as a wave of weakness washed over me. I felt dizzy for a moment and had to reach out to steady myself.

What if they reneged, I wondered. Refused to feed us. What would we do then?

Thankfully, just as Ryan was slipping back into his shirt I saw him slip his pistol into his jacket pocket when the back door opened. Mr. And Mrs. Farmer stepped out. He held his rifle in one hand. A Dutch oven by the metal handle in the other, she held a tray with five bowls and spoons.

"Chili and rice," she said with a sad smile. I thanked her as she handed me a bowl with about a cup of rice then him when he dolloped a huge ladle full of steaming chili over the rice. My insides gurgled with anticipation.

"Go slow," Ryan whispered.

"We've got dry dog food for your dog," She said as she ran into the house and came back with a tin plate heaped high with dry dog food.

I couldn't hold off and shoved a huge spoonful in and sighed with ecstasy. Oh, it tasted so good. The others quickly scarfed down their bowl then looked up. Old man Herman shook his head but he sighed then filled our bowls with more chili.

"Thank you," Ryan said around a mouthful of food as he reached over and ruffled Jake's fur. "You made a difference."

The old man stepped back, never letting the rifle drop too far. "You can sleep in the barn. Ain't got any chickens for you to steal. But you can't stay. Don't got enough food ourselves."

Ryan nodded. "Thank you. We can't stay anyway, got to get these guys to their families."

The old man nodded then escorted his wife back into the house. The loud click of the lock turning reminded me that these were nice people. We were the danger in their eyes.

We found a nice spot in the barn. Dry hay. Somehow we ended up in the same configuration as the night before. Paul and Ryan on the ends. Me next to Ryan. I wanted to spend some time talking, maybe just rest and recharge my batteries. But I was just too tired and too full. I ended up falling asleep before I could fully enjoy being held by Ryan.

The next morning I woke to a soft rain hitting the barn roof. I sat up and saw Ryan at the door looking out. Something about his body language told me he was feeling the weight of the world on his shoulders.

I got up to stand next to him. He glanced down and tried to give me a smile, but it didn't reach his eyes. Without thinking, I wrapped my arm around him and said. "We'll make it. I just know it."

He didn't laugh, didn't scoff, but I could see it in his eyes. He didn't believe me.

Chapter Twelve

Ryan

We'd just reached the front yard fence when the door opened behind us and the old woman rushed outside.

"Here," she said as she held out something wrapped in as red and white checkered tea towel.

My stomach clenched when I pulled a corner back to see five fluffy biscuits. "I wish it could be more." She said with a sad smile.

"Thank you," I said as I bit back a gulp of guilt. We were taking these people's food. How much did they have? Where would they get more? But I also knew this might make the difference.

She smiled then backed off and waited for us to leave.

The others glanced at me then at the precious bundle. "Lunch," I told them.

When we hit I-90 we headed east, each lost in our own world. The morning misty rain had stopped but the sky remained gray and threatening. We continued to check each car but we always came up empty.

When I heard Tania's stomach grumble I just couldn't put it off any longer and handed out a biscuit to each of them. I broke a corner off mine and held it out for Jake. Julia immediately did the same. Then Tania and Kelsey followed. Paul hesitated for a moment but he finally broke down and gave Jake a small piece.

My heart ached. I knew how much their stomachs hurt. That constant empty feeling but they'd sacrificed for my dog. It made me feel small and humble.

We continued on, no one talking, each saving our energy. Yes, we'd had a big meal the night before. At least big compared to recent days. But we had been so empty for so long that we needed more food just to get back to even.

Fat, my body screamed at me. We needed fat. A need for a sloppy hamburger refused to leave me. Filling me with a burning need.

We were a couple of miles down the road when we saw a group of about twenty people walking west on the other side of the highway. Without thinking I adjusted the Barretta in my waistband just to make sure it could come out quick and easy.

They looked like us. Travelers. Jeans, suits, no heavy jackets, no backpacks. But it was the eyes that hit me the hardest. Frightened, tired, about to give up. Did we look like that?

As we drew closer, an older man in a sports coat waved his hand and yelled, "There ain't nothing that way."

I wanted to tell him there wasn't much in front of him but I just shrugged. I didn't need to get into an argument over something that wasn't going to make any difference.

The other people kept walking, we kept walking. Two ships passing each other. To be forgotten and dismissed.

Kelsey fell back to walk with me. She shot me a quick smile and said, "We just keep moving. Right? We'll get there eventually."

I laughed. "We don't if we stop."

She smiled back at me and we continued on in a comfortable silence. Things had changed between us, I realized. We could be silent with each other and not worry about what the other was thinking. The friend zone, I realized with a touch of sadness.

But then what should I expect? If the world hadn't ended, we never would have known each other. We would have been two people sharing separate worlds. We had been thrown together not by choice but by circumstances. I guess we were lucky that we could at least be friends.

Sighing to myself, I put it aside. Focus on getting them there. That was all that was important. I could deal with my regrets, with what might have been, later.

We were about two miles out from the next town when we came across a group of people on the side of the road. It looked like two families. Two men, two women, seven kids from five to fifteen.

As we got closer the adults stared at us, silently warning us off. They had a fire going and a large pot boiling with stew. The savory smell of cooked meat hit me like a 2X4 upside the head. A jealous anger filled me. Where had they gotten the meat?

I was about to ask them when I saw one of the younger girls silently crying, holding a leash and an empty dog collar. My gut tightened with revulsion as I instinctively tightened my hold on Jake's leash.

My people stared at them. Kelsey reached over and patted Jake's side.

We kept walking, giving them a nod of greeting but not stopping to talk. I understood what had happened, but that didn't mean I could forgive. It had been ten days. Could things really be that bad already?

Kelsey glanced over at me with a tear in her eye and I knew she was thinking the same thing.

What would I do? No never. But could I be sure? I mean, this hunger burning a hole in my stomach made a person look at the world differently. If it had been my kid starving to death? Would my morals still be the same?

Thankfully we worked our way out of the smell of the stew and kept on to town. Unfortunately, as we approached we were greeted by a wooden barricade and four men guarding it with rifles.

A cop held up his hand for us to stop. "We aren't letting anyone in," he said with a tone of voice that let me know he wasn't going to change his mind.

"We just want to go through. We won't stop." I said. "We're going to Spokane."

He studied us for a long time. Five scraggly kids and a dog. I could see it in his eyes. We were a burden. A burden that would need to be fed.

"Nobody means nobody."

I bit my back teeth to stop from yelling at him. I was so frustrated. It was like everything was organized against us, stopping us from getting where we needed to go.

"Can we go around?" I asked as I fought to keep control.

He shrugged. "Just don't come into town. All the roads are blocked. You'll be shot if you try."

I swallowed hard as I glanced out at the muddy fields. I looked over the cop's shoulder at the small town. Two dozen buildings and six grain silos. Of course, I realized. They had something worth guarding. It was late in the growing year, this year's crop of winter wheat two months from harvest, and the silos were probably mostly empty. The grain long shipped off. But there would be some left. Enough to keep a small town going for a while.

"Go back about a mile," he said, "Take route 112 north, up two miles there's a crossroad, Maynard, head east, you'll find a route back to 90. Just don't come close to town. Somebody might shoot before reminding you to stay away. We had a group try from the west." He paused for a moment as he looked down. Then looked up and said, "They didn't make it."

My heart jumped as I imagined people so hungry they were willing to charge armed men. Then it clenched as I thought about walking back towards the people cooking by the side of the road. But we should be able to get off the road before we saw them.

I nodded at the man then asked. "How about east of here? Are the other towns doing this?"

He shrugged. "We haven't had any contact with anyone since this thing went down. No state people. There was an army group going through. But they didn't know anything. They were out on a training mission and got stuck. They were heading back to their base. But they didn't know anything. They did say the west coast is wiped out."

"Yes," I told him. "That's where we are from. We saw it."

"You walked all the way here?" his shocked tone said it all.

I shrugged then said, "Yes, and we'll end up walking all the way to Spokane."

His eyebrows rose in admiration then he shrugged and said, "Maybe, but it won't be through this town."

It took us two hours to work our way around the town. Two hours of wasted effort. Two hours worth of calories. But we were rewarded with the finest gift in the history of gifts.

We were a quarter mile from getting back to I-90 when Julia suddenly yelled and pointed. I whipped around to see a doe stuck in the mud forty feet from the road. She was struggling to break free. I could see what had happened. She'd traveled her normal path, but the field of alfalfa had become a quagmire that had entrapped her.

She was caked in brown mud and looked exhausted. Like she'd been fighting for hours.

My first instinct was to look around and make sure no one outside of our group had spotted this treasure. I pulled my pistol and started down the road bank.

"What are you doing?" Kelsey hissed.

I glanced back with a furrowed brown. "Getting dinner."

She frowned at me. I could see her battling with herself. A lifetime of easy living told her this wasn't necessary. A few days of hunger told her it was.

Ignoring her, I focused on doing what needed to be done. But I had to admit, I felt a twinge of guilt. Papa had always told me that taking a doe was wrong. But I convinced myself that she wasn't going to make it anyway. And we needed the food.

I had to wade through the mud to make sure I got close enough. The shot sounded louder than I expected. It took both me and Paul working our butts off to get the dead doe out of the mud and back up onto the road.

I did the best I could dressing it out. Papa had taught me that first summer we went deer hunting. My hand actually shook with anticipation as my mind couldn't stop thinking about cooked meat.

Both Tania and Julia held back shooting me looks of disgust. I'd just killed Bambi's mother. But I knew they'd change their minds when we started cooking.

Once I had harvested everything I could, I wrapped it up in the skin and threw it over my shoulder. Maybe forty pounds of meat, I thought as a sense of satisfaction filled me. We went back about a mile to a swollen creek lined with cottonwood trees.

Far enough away from the main road that people shouldn't smell the food.

"We'll camp here a couple of days," I told them. "Rest up."

That night we roasted strips of venison like hotdogs and gorged ourselves. I cooked up the organs for Jake. The next morning I found some wild onions down by the creek and roasted the bones directly on the fire then used them to cook up a stew, well mostly broth, but I wanted to make the meat last.

Everyone just laid around resting while I used the tarp to cover the fire and smoked a bunch of the meat. When it was done I wrapped it up in the tea towel and sighed. Two more days at least. We could stretch it into three.

We were sitting around the fire that evening when Kelsey sat down next to me and shot me a warm smile.

"What?" I asked, suddenly suspicious.

She laughed and shook her head. "Nothing. But isn't amazing how little it takes to make a person happy."

I nodded. "It's all about expectations, I guess. People always seem to want more."

"Well," she said, "We now know what is important. A full stomach. Safety. A place to hide from the rain. Friends to share it with."

I turned to see her staring at me intently. I swear there was some hidden message behind her eyes but I was clueless. Figuring out what girls thought was impossible. My sister and cousin had taught me that years ago. But her look made my insides tingle.

We held that look for a long moment but we were broken out of it by Julia suddenly coming and sitting on the other side of me and asking, "Are we going to go tomorrow?"

I forced my eyes away from Kelsey but not before I saw a hint of annoyance.

"Yes," I said. "I'll try and fish the creek in the morning. First light. Keep the meat for the trail."

Julia nodded then sighed heavily.

I smiled at her then felt Kelsey get up. I swear she stomped off. But I was sure I was wrong.

Chapter Thirteen

Kelsey

Walking became our world. Endless steps. One in front of the other. Always with a hunger eating at our stomachs.

Ryan was a rock of course. Leading from behind. It took me a while to understand that he always walked behind the group. Making sure to keep us together. Like a sheepdog. That was Ryan to a T. A guard dog by nature. Like Jake, a natural shepherd worried about his flock.

We had just passed through a small farm town when he suddenly yelled for us to hold up and pointed to a house just off the road. The front door was open, the dark windows were broken. And it looked like it was peppered with three bullet holes.

"Let's check it out," he said as he stepped down off the road towards the house. I hurried to catch up, making sure the others came. He paused outside, staring into the dark hole leading into the house. "Hello," he called then twisted to listen.

"Stay here," he said as he handed me Jake's leash.

"Why?" I demanded. I wanted to explore, do something that might make a difference. Mainly, I had a burning need to act instead of always reacting.

His brow furrowed, "Take a deep breath."

I frowned for a second then did what he asked and caught the sweet smell of rotting meat. I glanced at him wondering why that was significant then realized. Bodies. Regular eating meat would have been scavenged long ago.

Gasping, I stepped back, making sure the kids didn't get any closer. Ryan took a deep breath then yelled, "Hello," again before poking his head into the house. He shot us a quick look over his shoulder before stepping into the darkness and disappearing.

A thousand fears raced through me. Someone sitting in the dark with a shotgun. Diseases. Ghosts springing up from the dead. The full gamut.

Of course, he took half of forever to come back out with a pillowcase over his shoulder. My heart jumped at seeing him.

"No food," he said. Four faces fell with disappointment but he gave us a small smile." I found a salt and pepper set. Another pot, and plastic plates. Forks. And another blanket. It was at the bottom of a linen closet and got missed."

I desperately wanted to ask about if he found anybody but I could tell by the sadness around his eyes that he had. I could also tell he didn't want to talk about it. One more of those times when a boy refused to discuss his emotions.

His way of keeping pain away from us, I realized. He'd take it on and carry it all alone. Without thinking, I reached out and caressed his shoulder and gave him a look that let him know I appreciated him.

I swear it was like I'd given him the best present ever. He smiled back at me with genuine thanks. His smile hit me hard as I realized just how much I worried about him. And more importantly. How much I needed him to worry about me. Not just as a friend but as the most important person in his world.

That was when the idea of love began to sneak into my soul. Was I in love with Ryan Conrad? No. Impossible. But really, why wouldn't I be? I mean, the guy was way cute. A rock in an emergency. A relentless worker. A guardian. Oh yeah, he'd saved my life more than once.

Yes, just maybe I was in love with him.

A new sadness hit me as we started down the road. He wasn't in love with me. At least not from what I could see. I mean he'd never shown any of the signs. No flirting. No chasing. No empty compliments. I mean, wasn't that what boys did when they wanted someone?

Suddenly I began to question everything I knew as a new hope began to build inside of me. Maybe Ryan wasn't like other boys. I laughed at the thought.

"What?" he asked me, glancing over with a deep frown.

I couldn't stop smiling at the thought of Ryan being like other boys. No boy was more different. At least not in my world. I simply waved my hand in dismissal. No way was I telling him that I was thinking about him and how special he was.

And still, we walked, one step in front of the other. Eastern Washington was so different from home. Flat. I mean, with a real horizon and everything. You could see twenty miles in every direction. And no trees.

Hey, I was a Western Washington girl. That meant trees were a permanent part of my life. Every road was lined with tall sentinels. The forest was dark and deep. The air always smelled of pine and there was a feeling of life.

Even the city, Once you got out you were immediately in the forest. The distant mountains were covered in trees.

It was so different on this side. Just flatness forever. Farms, now covered in mud. Crops destroyed and the feeling of an endless openness.

It rained in the afternoon and we ducked into a mini-van for an hour. It was like that every day. At least some rain. Ryan said that the asteroid had changed the weather patterns. Thrown so much energy and water up into the atmosphere it might be a year before it got back to normal.

We shared some of the venison then settled in to wait out the rain. I sighed heavily and stared at the rain running down the window. Every so often I would glance over at Ryan who had leaned in the corner with his eyes closed.

Was this feeling because he had saved my life? I mean, was that all it was? Would I feel this way towards any boy who had saved me?

Pulling it out, I examined it and had to admit that maybe a part of it was because he saved my life. But then wasn't that sort of normal? The whole princess being saved by the prince. There was a reason why those stories resonated so much.

But there was more. So much more to Ryan. Kindness, a key to the whole thing. Yes, I remembered all those people we had passed. He'd warned them, but hadn't let that slow us. Again, I knew deep in my heart part of the reason was his determination to save me.

I kept coming back to that.

Maybe I was just being a fool. Overthinking things. Or worse, wasting my emotions thinking about something that would never happen. Not the first time, I thought as I remembered fantasies about my Dad coming back to me.

Was that it? Did I have Daddy issues? I'd fallen for the first guy to protect and provide for me.

Jesus Kelsey, I thought to myself as I realized just how screwed up I was. No wonder Ryan didn't pay me any attention.

Ryan opened his eyes and stared out at the rain. "We'll just stay here tonight."

My heart fell as I realized I wouldn't get to sleep curled up next to him tonight. We'd be in our separate seats. But I kept my thoughts to myself.

The rain stopped just after the sun went down. I pulled the blanket up to my chin and let myself go to sleep as I continued to try and figure out the mystery known as Ryan Conrad.

I woke to Ryan yelling and Jake barking his head off. My heart jumped to my throat as I saw Ryan fighting to hold the door closed as a man pulled at it. The silver moonlight showed a man in his forties fighting to get into the van.

Suddenly, Ryan yelled and instead of pulling the door closed, he shoved it open and jumped out. The man was caught in the gut and taken off guard, falling back to land on his butt. Almost instantly Ryan was over him with the pistol drawn and pointed at the man's head. His finger slowly squeezing the trigger.

"Ryan," I gasped as I scrambled over into his seat then out the door, terrified he was going to shoot the man.

He froze, staring down at his advisory. The man lay, supported by his elbows, his brow narrowed in anger. "Go ahead Kid," he cursed. "Get it over with. We're all dead anyway."

My world stopped as I tried to understand what was happening. The man looked gaunt with hollow cheeks. I wondered when was the last time he had eaten.

"What do you want?" Ryan yelled as he fought to maintain control. "We don't have any food," he lied. I thought about our venison and wondered if she should give some to this man. Then I thought about the kids. Suddenly I realized that we couldn't feed the world. Not and survive.

The man's glare narrowed as he stared up at the pistol pointing at him. Finally, he sighed and nodded. "Okay." He gave Ryan another glance then turned over to push himself up.

Ryan never wavered, keeping the pistol pointed at the man's chest. "Just move on." He said, nodding for the man to keep going down the road.

The man hesitated for a moment then nodded and started away. Ryan twisted to follow him until he disappeared into the darkness.

"Jake,"

The dog growled deep in his chest as he looked into the darkness where the man had disappeared.

"Get our stuff," Ryan said to us without lowering his weapon or looking away.

We scrambled to get our belongings and were lined up ready to go in about two minutes. One of the benefits of not having anything.

"We'll go down and find a place to camp," Ryan said as he pulled at Jake's leash to break him away from his guard duties.

An hour later we found a small creek, again, swollen like every other creek in the world but we were able to find a bend that would hide us from the road and two small scraggly trees for the tarp turned tent.

I had to smile to myself. I would get to sleep next to Ryan after all.

We ran out of smoked venison the next day. The day after a burning hunger returned. But still, we walked. Maybe ten or fifteen miles a day. We might have been able to do more. But no food takes energy out of a person and we were dragging.

We were setting up camp on the second day of no food when Ryan stopped and stared at the distant fields.

"What?" I asked him.

He shook his head and returned to helping string the tarp.

That night a silence fell over us as we each stared into the fire. I knew the others were thinking about the venison we had cooked over the fire and that mouthwatering savory smell that satisfied a soul. Paul and Julia were thinking about camping trips and roasting marshmallows. Tania was probably remembering that special dinner with her dad.

A depression hit me. Was this the end of us? If not today. Maybe in a week or so. We couldn't get all the way to Spokane without food. Had we fought so hard only to fail?

I glanced over at Ryan to find him staring off into the night. Suddenly he got up and got the pillow case and dumped out all our stuff. We hadn't anything to cook so we'd never emptied it.

"Stay here," he demanded as he started off into the night.

"What? Why?" I called after him, furious that he treated us, me, like we weren't important enough to know what he was doing.

"I'll let you know. If this works." And he was gone.

Rolling my eyes I actually stomped my foot.

"Don't be mad at Ryan," Julia said with a possessive tone that just pissed me off even more.

"Listen, little girl," I snapped. "Don't tell me who to be mad at or not. You're not old enough to understand."

I swear, it was like I'd slapped her. I'd crossed a line and accused her of the worst thing imaginable. Being too young. But I didn't care. I was just too furious to worry about Julia's feelings.

She stared at me then stomped off into the dark. "Go after her," I said to Paul. "Before she gets lost and we spend the next two days searching for her."

He gave me a quick glare then followed his sister into the night.

Tania shot me a look before shaking her head.

"What?" I demanded while I heard a distant noise and wondered if Ryan was coming back.

"Jealousy isn't a good look for you."

I scoffed, "Jealous of Julia. Are you kidding me? Why would I be jealous of a little kid?"

She stared at me for a long moment then shook her head, obviously aware she was dealing with an idiot. "Ryan doesn't think of her that way. Special. As girl friend material. And she's scared out of her mind. So cut her some slack."

The anger inside of me just wouldn't ease off so I said, "Why would I care what Ryan thought."

She laughed and said, "Because you are in love with him. And what makes it worse? He's in love with you. But you're both too dumb to see it."

I could only stare at her as I fought to stop as charging hope from filling me. Could she be right? No. Impossible. But still a hope ate at the edges of my certainty.

Then a sudden rifle shot echoing through the night brought my terrible world back to me.

Chapter Fourteen

Ryan

Okay, maybe not the smartest move. But it was just too good to pass up. I'd spotted a sodden wheatfield when we set up camp. Bent stalks soaking in the mud. But, in the far corner on a piece of slightly higher ground, a clump of wheat not beaten into the ground.

Winter wheat that should be harvested in a couple of weeks. I didn't want to say anything just in case this didn't work. I'd noticed that every time they got their hearts broken, it took longer and longer to bounce back.

They were dragging, fighting over the littlest thing. The constant gnawing emptiness of our stomachs torturing us endlessly. I'd heard Julia crying in her sleep last night. One more heartbreak might be too much.

So I snuck into the night, letting my eyes adjust to the dark. The clouds had parted a bit letting in enough starlight to work my way around the edge of the field. I had to slide through a barbed wire fence, cutting my thumb but I ignored the pain as I focused on what I needed to do. The field had that molding wet smell that turned a person's stomach.

This will work, I kept telling myself as I slogged through the mud to the dry patch.

Once I got there I fell to my knees and used my buck knife to start harvesting the wheat, cutting the heads off at the top of the stem and stuffing them into the pillow case.

I was thrilled that I was getting so much when the night exploded with a very loud and very close rifle shot.

Doing the only smart thing, I fell to my gut and crawled out of there, dragging the bag full of wheat behind me. I'd made about fifty feet and stopped to catch my breath, fighting to control my racing heart, while listening but the pounding blood in my ears made it impossible. Someone could be driving a tank six feet away and I wouldn't have heard them.

Obviously. Some farmer didn't want anyone stealing his food. I couldn't blame him. But I had people starving. And I needed to get those people away before we were discovered. The fire was hidden. But the wind was right so he might smell the smoke.

Taking a deep breath, I pushed up and began to run, bent at the waist, expecting a slug to the back at any moment. Thankfully, the clouds shifted and hid the faint starlight. Giving me time to make the camp.

Kelsey stared at me with wide eyes. Jake jumped on me, welcoming me back to the pack.

"Where's Paul and Julia?" I asked as I frantically began to kick dirt over the fire.

"Here," Paul said as he and Julia stepped out of the dark.

"What is going on?" Kelsey demanded, giving me a look like she wanted to chew me out for the next two weeks.

"We need to go," I hissed then began taking down the tarp. "Grab the stuff and let's go."

All four of them stared back, unable to process what was happening. "Now," I growled, snapping them into action. Two minutes later we were on the road, once more headed east.

"What happened," Kelsey insisted, "And what is in the bag?"

"Food," I answered, shaking the pillow case, "At least I hope so. And someone didn't want me to have it."

The darkness hid her scowl but I knew it was there. "You shouldn't do that," she hissed. "Risk yourself."

"Kelsey," I sighed, frustrated. "We don't have a choice. This is our new world. You risk or you die."

We continued on for a moment then I asked. "Why is Julia upset?"

She growled and said, "I don't want to talk about it."

"Fine," I answered, pleased I didn't have to solve another problem.

Later that morning, as the sun came up, I realized we had crossed out of the farm country and into desert. You knew it was desert because it was full of sagebrush, rocks, and sand. My gut tightened with emptiness and I knew the other's were hurting. "Let's find a place to stop," I told them.

A dry ravine was the perfect spot. The bottom still held muddy puddles but we could work our way around them to behind a bend, cut off from the road. We set up the tarp, tying it off between two rocks on either side of the ravine. It would keep either the sun or the rain off of us.

We spent the morning working the wheat. First beating it so the kernels came loose, then rubbing them and tossing them for the wind to winnow away the chaff. We ended up with almost two pounds that we crushed between two flat stones.

"We really are back in the stone age," Paul said. One of his common refrains.

"Yeah," I said, "But without generations of knowledge. We are going to have to learn all over."

Kelsey mixed the flour with water and cooked up tortillas. Or sort of tortillas. They were drab but they filled a person's stomach and we had enough for tomorrow's meal.

"How much farther?" Tania asked as we leaned back with semi-full bellies.

"Maybe forty miles. Three days."

They silently looked down and I knew what was going through their minds. What would they find when they got home?

Kelsey could see it too and said, "Your mom is going to be so pleased to see you."

Tania shook her head. "I live with my grandparents. I was supposed to move to my mom's in Portland next year."

"You were?" Paul asked with wide eyes. "Why didn't you tell us that?"

Tania shook her head. "It doesn't matter now. Does it? Would Portland have survived?"

"It might have," I told her trying to ease her pain, "The coast mountains might have blocked the tsunami."

She shrugged. "It doesn't matter. She would never come back here. There isn't anything important enough to make that trip."

My stomach clenched with sorrow. What must her life have been like to think like that? I had been so lucky. Yes, Mom had died, but I knew she loved me. And Dad had tried to fill both roles. I couldn't imagine it being otherwise.

Kelsey draped an arm around her shoulder and gave her a quick hug.

Julia said, "Our Mom and Dad will have food and can feed everyone. In fact, Ryan. You should think about staying with us instead of going to your grandfather's."

I gave her my best smile and said, "My Papa is expecting me. I can't disappoint him."

Her face fell and my heart hurt. I knew she had a crush on me. I'm not oblivious. Thankfully Kelsey stood up and pushed at her lower back. "When I find my Mom, I am going to sleep in a real bed."

We all laughed and once again we were a team with a common goal. Getting our people back where they belonged.

Two days later, I sort of began to rethink everything. We were approaching Cheney when we saw the first body hanging from a telephone pole with a sign around his neck that read, THIEF.

We froze, unable to believe it as he dangled in the wind. Who was he? I wondered then thought about all the things we had stolen along the way. Looting, breaking into houses, the wheat field.

"Why did they leave him up there?" Paul asked in shock.

"A warning," I said as my insides tightened.

"It's gross," Kelsey said, unable to look away.

It looked like the man had been there for a few days. He was heavyset with a leather jacket with some kind of patch on the back. "Come on," I said as I motioned for them to keep going. I was still trying to put the picture of that guy out of my mind when we came across another man swinging in the breeze.

Once was happenstance, two, then three was a pattern that said so much. I made sure to shift the pillow case to my left hand so I could draw my pistol if necessary.

"How much further," I asked. I wanted to get these kids back to their guardians. I'll be honest, I was going to miss them. But I wasn't going to miss the responsibility.

"A mile, I think," Tania said. "On the right."

A mile, I thought. What would happen after that? I'd get Kelsey to her mom, then I was on my own. Just me and Jake. A sadness washed through me at the thought. How had this happened? Two weeks earlier, I was a loner. A guy without friends. Now, these people were like family. The thought of just walking away didn't seem right.

Especially Kelsey.

Sometimes, I'd catch her giving me strange looks from beneath her brow. She'd quickly look away but not before I saw something in her eyes, a sad, lonely look that tore at my heart.

We eventually turned off onto a side road into a suburban housing development. Cheney was a bedroom community for Spokane. Maybe twelve thousand people, plus another four thousand when the college kids were in school. A small town with that small-town feel.

Tania pointed to a house a block down. Several people pulled blinds back to see who was coming up their street.

"Hi Mrs. Sinclair," Tania yelled as she waved at an older woman stepping out onto her porch. The woman didn't wave back, just watched, glancing behind us, searching for trouble. My heart fell as a sense of foreboding filled me. The others didn't catch it though as their steps quickened.

As we approached Tania's house my stomach fell. The place was darker than a dungeon.

"Gramps," Tania yelled as she opened the door. "Nana."

The deathly silence filled me with sadness. The place looked deserted. A layer of dust on the coffee table, a musky scent, like a tomb. No death smell I realized. No bodies in the back room. Thank God.

Tania froze with her hand on the door then rushed into the house calling for her grandparents.

Kelsey put a hand on my arm, her eyes terrified at what our friend was going to find. We both stood there waiting until Tania came back, her eyes wide in shock. "They're not here."

I could only grimace, the pain in her face was heart-wrenching. She'd spent the last two weeks dreaming of this moment only to have it dashed.

"You can come to our house," Julia said as she gave her friend a hug. "Isn't that right, Paul?"

He hesitated, obviously in shock then said, "Yes, of course. Maybe my mom or dad will know where they went."

Tania looked like her mind was whirling a mile a minute as she tried to understand. Once again her world had changed in a bad way.

Pushing past them I went to the kitchen and started opening cupboards. Gone, every scrap of food was gone. Had they taken it with them? Had raiders came in and taken it? All I knew was my stomach clenched in disappointment.

"Come on," I said to them. "Let's go to Paul's and Julia's."

Tania stared at nothing, unable to move, unable to make a decision.

"You can't stay here," I told her as I put my arm around her shoulder and pulled her close. "There isn't any food. We can come back."

She looked up at me with misty eyes then nodded, unable to say the words. I gently led her out of the house.

Paul replaced me, holding her, leading her. Julia gave us instructions. Basically up two blocks and over one.

We were almost there when the clop of horseshoes on pavement made us all freeze and turn around. Three men approached, each with a rifle at the ready. An older guy up front. Two teenagers on either side. My stomach clenched as my hand itched to pull my pistol. But, I'm not a complete fool and stopped myself.

"You lot," the leader said, "Where you going? You know the rules."

"What rules," I asked. "We just came here, from Seattle." I pointed to the kids. "They live here. I'm bringing them back to their parents."

"Seattle?" the guy said with disbelief. "No way."

Two weeks of frustration and anger bubbled out before I could stop it. "Why would we lie about that? We were there, now we're here."

His brow furrowed and I could see it instantly, dumb, and filled with power. Probably for the first time in his life. Dumb and powerful is never a good combination.

"Hey Jeff," one of the younger guys said, kneeing his horse to advance up next to the leader. "I know her," he pointed to Tania. "She lives on my street. And I'm pretty sure those other two are the Carlson twins. You know their Dad was killed at the station fight."

Both Paul and Julia gasped. The shock in their eyes would haunt me forever.

"NO!" Paul yelled as he turned and raced towards his home.

My heart went out to him as my heart was filled with anger. At least the young guy had the good sense to look guilty. I put him out of my mind. I needed to know, "What rule?"

The leader looked at Paul running up the street then at Julia crying in Kelsey's arms. He took a deep breath then said, "No raiding other people's houses."

"Let me guess," I said. "Getting caught can end up with a person hanging from a telephone pole."

He scoffed, "No, that we reserve for outsiders from Spokane who come here to take what is ours. General thieves we just shoot on sight."

Chapter Fifteen

Kelsey

Julia cried in my arms then suddenly broke away and raced for her house. I shot Ryan a look filled with disappointment and pure pain.

He sighed heavily and shook his head. I knew he was hurting. He'd lost his mom, he knew their pain. I guy like Ryan just took on the world's problems. If it was broken he needed to fix it. But he would never understand that some things can never be fixed.

The three horsemen watched as Paul's mother opened the door then collapsed in shock. It seemed to be the confirmation they needed as the leader spun away.

A sadness filled me. Would it ever end? The constant devastation. Families ruined, lives snuffed out. Why? For the thousandth time, I realized just how good we had it before. How perfect our world had been. Yes, we had fought and argued about stupid things. Things that really weren't that important when compared to surviving.

The youngest rider, the one who knew Tania, slid down off his horse and gave us a sad look. The guy might have been fifteen. But something around his eyes told me he'd stopped being a kid a couple of weeks ago. Like the rest of us, he had grown up fast.

"I'm Dylan Southerland," he said as way of introduction.

We watched as Paul, Julia, and their mom hugged, laying on the door step, crying into each other's arms.

"What happened, at the station," Ryan asked the rider.

The kid took a deep breath and shook his head. "Things got bad." The sadness in his voice tore at me. "When the stuff stopped, a train was passing through town, just past the rail station. A couple of the cars were full of corn. The last of last year's harvest."

"That's lucky," Ryan said.

Dylan shrugged, "Maybe, but a bunch of men came out of Spokane and took it. Or took control of it. Maybe two hundred. All armed. I think they were gang members, bikers who got kicked out of Spokane."

Ryan winced.

The kid sighed heavily again. "Chief Spencer. The Sheriff, organized a group. Basically all the men and got it back. It took us two days."

He paused, obviously remembering the fight. My heart went out to him. A fifteen-year-old boy shouldn't be put in that situation. Nobody should.

"We finally got them all. Those we captured alive ... they were hung. But out of the two hundred, we maybe only got a dozen. The men, they didn't take prisoners. We'd lost too many."

"Mr. Carlson didn't make it?"

Dylan shook is head. "We lost as many as we killed. We didn't have a choice. That corn was ours."

My stomach clenched as I realized what the world had become. Kill or be killed. Protect your own no matter what.

"What's Spokane like?" Ryan asked.

Dylan scoffed and shook his head. "I hear it's become a hell hole. Literally. Broken up by different groups. You can't move from one to the other. People scrambling for food. The Chief said it's like one of those old-fashioned cities under siege. Only there isn't an enemy at the gate. People can leave. But where are they going to go? And they can't take their food with them. The gangs won't let them."

I cringed inside. Mom was in the middle of all that.

"Let's go say goodbye to them," Ryan said, nodding to the family still grieving at the door. As we approached I felt Ryan take a deep breath and say. "Mrs. Carlson, I'm Ryan Conrad. I'm sorry."

The woman looked up and I was shocked. She looked haggard, thin, with hollow cheeks and eyes that looked like they'd cried for years. Her jeans and T-shirt hung on her like loose sails in a dead calm. She frowned as she fought to bring herself back to reality.

"Mom," Paul said as he broke away from his mother. "This is Ryan and Kelsey. They saved us and got us home."

The older woman continued to frown then said, "You should have stayed away."

My jaw dropped. How could a mother say that? But the fear in the woman's eyes fought with a soul-searing relief at having her children. The conflict inside this woman was taring her apart.

"Come in," she said as she hugged her children and led the way into the house. I shot Ryan a worried look then followed the family into a typical suburban home. No lights of course but enough came in through the windows to see clean, nice furniture.

Mrs. Carlson led us into the kitchen. Ryan placed the pillowcase on the dinning room table and waited. That said so much about him. His patience. His ability to wait and see. He'd let it play out then take action.

I on the other hand wanted to ask a dozen questions. To press her about why she wished her children had stayed away.

"I don't have much," she said as she started opening cupboards. "Cornmeal of course. Some Peanut butter, Almonds. Because of your father ... I get a ration every few days. We have to go to the station. They keep track. But I kept a jar of olives, my emergency food. I was going to start a garden in the back. But ..."

A deep despondency filled me. The woman looked so beat. She'd lost her husband. Thought she'd lost her children. Been starved with barely enough to survive on. Of course she looked beaten.

"Why?" Ryan asked. "Why did you wish that Paul and Julia hadn't come back."

A tear began to slowly fall as she quickly wiped at her eyes. "I shouldn't have said that." She pulled her children in for another hug, obviously unable to not touch them. "But things aren't good here."

"There not good anywhere," Ryan said.

She nodded, "I know. But I think they are going to get even worse. Spokane is falling apart. People keep coming. Searching for food. There have been shootings. To try and stop them."

I gasped. Ryan's brow narrowed. "We were lucky we came in from the other direction."

She sighed then looked at her children and broke down crying again as she pulled them into a hug. "Your father ..." She clenched her jaw to stop from crying more. "He would have been so proud of you. He said we needed to survive so we would be here when you came home."

Tania stepped forward. "Do you know what happened to my grandparents?"

Mrs. Carlson's eyes grew sadder as she shook her head. "People are desperate. Maybe they went somewhere looking for food. Or. I don't know. I'm sorry. But if they aren't there. I wouldn't expect them to come back."

Tania turned to cry on me as Ryan took a deep breath and said. "Tania is coming with us. We have to stop in Spokane and get Kelsey's mom. Then we're going to my Grandfather's farm in Norther Idaho. You're welcome to come with us."

My heart soared as I smiled at him, so proud of him. He was taking on more responsibilities. We hadn't talked about it but I knew he had been looking forward to handing off the duties of being caretaker, provider, and protector. But here he was, taking on more.

"You can't go into Spokane," she said as she looked at me with sadness. "A girl. The stories." She shuddered.

My heart fell. But I also knew I wasn't leaving my mom to that. Suddenly I realized Ryan had said, get my mom. That implied he was taking us with him. A bolt of love filled me. He wanted me to go with him.

"We have to try," he said. "You think about it. We need to stop at Tania's so she can leave a note for her grandparents. But we need to get going before things get worse.

A silent expectancy hung in the air as Mrs. Carlson looked at her children. "Please Mom," Julia said. "Dad would want us to go. To be safe."

Paul nodded. "We have to. The mountains, away from people. We need to be invisible."

I almost smiled as he used Ryan's expression.

She hesitated for a moment then nodded.

So that was how instead of losing three people we gained one more. Once the decision had been made Ryan took over. Organizing our supplies. Searching through the house for what we needed. Then I yelled when I discovered that the water faucets still worked.

"Ryan," I said as I rushed through the house to find him digging through Paul's closet. "Baths. I need a bath. We all do."

His frown looked more confused than angry but he let out a long sigh and nodded. "We can go in the morning. A night in real beds might be nice."

I squealed with happiness as I rushed out to tell the others. Thankfully, Mrs. Carlson had clothes I could have. Tania could wear Julia's. Even Ryan could wear clothes from Mr. Carlson. We spent the evening freshening up with cold water baths and eating corn tortillas with peanut butter.

Ryan laid out everything he wanted us to take. Two pots, eight plastic bowls, every scrape of food. Six blankets to be rolled up and slung over our shoulders. Two pocket knives he found, one for me, one for Paul. Three candles, a box of wooden matches. Ball caps. A change of clothes each. A roll of fishing line and some hooks. Our trusty tarp. Two twenty-foot lengths of rope he found in the garage. And most important, two rolls of toilet paper.

"Do you have a gun?" he asked Mrs. Carlson with a hopeful voice.

She shook her head. "My Jim had to borrow one. The sheriff's men kept it."

He nodded as he examined everything laid out on the dinning room table. It wasn't much, I realized. Paul came back with two old bookbags. One of them pink with Rainbow Dash. Julia blushed with embarrassment.

Ryan smiled. "Unfortunately we'll have to use them. They will be big enough for our stuff."

That night I slept in a real bed and felt lost. Tania was in Paul's room. I had Julia's. Mrs. Carlson insisted her children sleep with her that night. Ryan slept on the couch in the living room.

Like I said, I felt lost. I realized I would have exchanged that cloud of a mattress for the hard ground if it meant I got to sleep curled up next to Ryan. At the same time, my insides were constantly churning, worrying about my mother.

What was she going through? I knew that most cities only had two weeks' worth of food. But that was the average. That some people had months, others days. And Mom had been in a hotel. Had they fed her?

I lay there, unable to fall asleep, staring into the darkness.

"This is ridiculous," I said as I threw back my blankets and pulled on my clothes. "Ryan," I hissed as I stepped into the living room. "Are you awake?"

Jake lifted his head from the floor next to the couch, bouncing his tail in greeting.

"I am now," Ryan said as he sat up. "What's wrong."

"I can't sleep," I said as I caught him bare-chested. Those wide shoulders taking on the weight of the world. "I guess I'm too used to hard ground."

He snorted then scooted over so I could sit down next to him. I sat down and took in that delicious smell of soap and woodsmoke.

"Are you worried about your mom?"

I swallowed hard as I nodded then he did the one thing I wanted more than almost anything else in the world. He put his arm around me and held me close. Keeping the horrors away.

We sat there in silence, each taking energy and comfort in the other. Who was this boy? I wondered. I really knew so little about him. And yet, I think I knew more about him than anyone else in this world.

"Tell me something about yourself," I said. "From before. Something no one knows."

He laughed then said, "Ryan isn't my name."

"What?" I said as I pulled away so I could stare at him.

Smiling he shrugged. "Technically, it's Orion. My Dad's an astrophysicist, remember? And Cassie is really named Cassiopeia. You know, after the constellations. My cousin Haley is after the comment. Only Chase got a real name."

I could only stare at him then smiled to myself. I knew something about him that no one outside of his family knew. That made me special. Sighing I slipped back under his arm and lay my head in the crook of his arm and felt my world a little bit better.

Chapter Sixteen

Ryan

It was so strange walking with an adult in the group. A deeply bred instinct told me to let her take charge. She was the adult. But another part of me refused to give up control. Luckily, Mrs. Carlson didn't seem to want it. She just wanted to hold her kids.

We had loaded up. I wore one backpack, I made Paul wear the Rainbow Dash one. He shot his sister an evil stare but he shrugged into the straps without complaining. I then told him I wanted him to take the rear. I'd take the lead. "Don't let anyone get behind you. If necessary yell and I'll stop us. But your job is to herd them together."

"We're not sheep," Kelsey snapped. "Why does Paul have to do it?"

I sighed internally. No way was I getting into a fight about this. I mean the whole women and children get the lifeboats thing was way too real. So instead I just said, "Because that's the way I want it." Then turned and started down the road.

I could feel her rolling her eyes behind me but I ignored it and focused on getting us out of there.

So many things could go so wrong so fast. At first, I was constantly glancing over my shoulder to make sure they stayed close but as we worked our way through town we started seeing more people. Men on horseback with rifles. Individuals darting from shadow to shadow. A long line outside the train station.

"It's not my day for food," Mrs. Carlson said with a sadness.

I could see the constant fear in her eyes. She was leaving her home. She was leaving her dead husband and venturing out into the unknown. And now she had her children to worry about. The doubt must be eating her alive. But I think she could see the writing on the wall. Cities weren't going to make it.

Even if we had enough to last until harvest season. We didn't have the ability to grow the food needed. Simple things like tractors, combines, trucks bringing fertilizers. No mules to pull plows. And even if we had, they couldn't grow enough food. No, famine was the city's future. The best hope was in the mountains. Living off the land. Hunter-gatherers once more.

When we hit the edge of town we came up behind a barricade with two dozen men and a couple of younger women, each armed to the max, each focused on the road coming from Spokane. The leader broke off and came back towards us. I motioned for my people to hold back.

"What do you lot want? We've got enough people. See the Sherif's men if you want to work, they'll feed you."

I shook my head. "We're headed for Spokane."

His eyes widened then he barked out a short laugh. However, he quickly sobered when he realized I wasn't joking. "Not smart."

Shrugging, I motioned to Kelsey. "Her Mom is there."

He frowned, glanced at our backpacks, and I knew he was going to insist on searching them but then he glanced at my group and sighed heavily. "It's your funeral," he said as he motioned for his people to open a path through the barricade. I was also sure he had calculated, fewer people in his town meant more food.

But I knew it wasn't going to make a difference, these people were trapped and there was no solution.

I signaled for my people to hurry up. I didn't want this guy changing his mind. We slipped through the barrier and into a sparse section of the road.

Cheney, Spokane, and Coeur d'Alene are almost one long city separated by hamlets, subdivisions, and the occasional farm. We worked our way north to catch I-90. Once again we were greeted by bodies hanging from telephone poles.

All I did was grit my teeth and focus on getting us down the road. As we walked, I began to realize something. No people. No cows in the fields. It took me a bit to figure it out. The Spokane groups had swept through the area. Taking what they wanted, killing those who tried to stop them. They'd met a harsh end in Cheney.

For the thousandth time, I cursed the loss of vehicles. The Army couldn't respond. And even if they could, they would have been too late for most of those people alone away from Cheney.

Those that made it through had learned their lesson and stayed hidden. Invisible. And we were walking into a world where that would be impossible.

Kelsey scurried up to walk next to me. Excited but nervous. I could see the worry in her eyes. What would she find when we got there?

"You really are going to take my mom with us?"

I shrugged. "If she wants to come." There was no need to tell her that I had figured that it was the only way to get Kelsey to safety and somewhere along the road that had become the main goal of my life. Once I had her safely tucked away at my Papa's I could hit the road and find my sister.

She looked over her shoulder at Mrs. Carlson with her arm around Julia. I glanced over and smiled. "We did something good. Getting them back with their mother."

Kelsey nodded. "I just hope we did the right thing, taking them with us."

"We'll never know. I think that is what has changed so much. Before, we made a decision, and if it was wrong, we suffered public shame, maybe a financial hit. But we survived to fight another day. Now, the wrong decision gets people killed."

The reality of my words ate at my gut. But there was no pretending it wasn't so.

The gray clouds had parted letting in enough spring sun to start the drying out process. The air was almost humid, rare for Eastern Washington. We hit the city line just after noon. The weird smell that hit us made the back of my throat tickle. A sickly sweat smell that didn't make sense. Then when I saw the man dead in the gutter covered in flies I knew.

Bodies. Dead People. My stomach rebelled as I realized how many bodies it would take to create that much stink.

Kelsey covered her mouth and shot me a frightened look. I glanced over my shoulder and motioned for everyone to close up as I pulled my pistol.

We slowly moved forward, each of us scanning for danger. Of course, it came from where we didn't expect. From behind.

It was Jake who warned me, whipping around and barking at a group of people charging towards us. Maybe six or seven, a hundred yards back, all in their twenties and thirties, some with rifles, most with clubs or knives. All with that feral look of hunger-driven madness.

Why? I wondered. Food, I realized, they would take what they needed to survive.

"Run," I yelled as I waved my people towards the nearest off-ramp. Falling back, I kept myself between the group, holding Jake's leash in one hand, my pistol in the other.

"Ryan," Kelsey yelled as they reached the off-ramp.

I fired one shot over the pursuer's heads then turned and raced for my people. I think I slowed them down a dozen seconds or so. But the hunger in their guts overruled their fear as they started for us again.

We must have looked like easy targets. Mostly women and girls. Only one gun apparent, the dog on the leash. I cursed myself. We should have found more weapons. We should have done this at night.

We raced down off the ramp and rushed across the street to an alley. "Run," I yelled encouragingly as I heard their feet stomping down the ramp between us.

"Find a place to hide," I yelled to Kelsey who had taken the lead.

She glared at me with a frown as if that wasn't obvious. My people hadn't had a steady diet for weeks. They were winded easily. I could feel it myself. A few hundred yards and my side was punching a hole in my gut. What must the little ones be feeling?

Kelsey turned right, then left down another alley.

I was tempted to fall back and hold our chasers off but I was terrified I'd lose Kelsey and the others. In this maze of streets, I might never find them again.

Suddenly, Kelsey ducked in through the broken glass of a department store. She wove between circular stands of women's dresses, around a cosmetic counter, and then into a dark corner. I was going to tell her to keep going, we were trapped then saw the emergency exit door. The kind you couldn't get in from the outside.

She waved us down, behind a display of men's jeans.

We all crouched, Trying desperately to be quiet while sucking in air, fighting to slow our racing hearts.

Mrs. Carlson hugged her children to her like a mother hen. Kelsey held Tania, all of them looking at me like I had to save them.

I peeked around the edge of the display, my pistol ready, I'd decided if they came, I'd hold them off so my people could get away. I'd find them at the Davenport.

But our pursuers never showed. Somehow we'd lost them. I took a deep breath and slowly made my way to the front of the store, positive they were going to jump out of a shadow and take me down.

Peeking my head out of the broken windows I scanned the street. Thankfully they never showed up. Why? I mean they hadn't been that far behind. Had we truly lost them? Or was there something even more frightening around here? My gut told me it was the latter.

When I got back to my people I motioned for them to follow and led the way through the emergency exit. Be more careful, I told myself. No more walking down the middle of a major freeway. Instead, we hopped from shadowed storefront to alley garbage dumpster. Darting across streets when I was sure the coast was clear.

No one complained. They followed my lead, we didn't move until I was sure we were going to be safe.

It took us a couple of hours to work our way to where the Davenport was. Mrs. Carlson pointed the way. I guess she and her husband had spent a romantic weekend there years ago. We dropped down off I-90 and walked along the river, the loud rumble of the falls echoing off the buildings.

The river was a grayish mush, swollen at full flood levels. Up over its banks and rushing through the park. But the bridges looked good.

How long I wondered? If the river washed out the banks the roads would collapse and they'd never get fixed again.

As we walked I kept a close look out. There were some people in tents and makeshift shelters in the dry part of the park. Most of the buildings were businesses supporting the convention center.

My gut tightened as people stared at us as we walked, eyeing us like possible prey. I could see it, hopeless people, some with kids, desperate for help. I made a point of keeping my pistol drawn and visible.

"Around the next corner," Mrs. Carlson said as she pointed.

My heart stopped as we rounded a building, there, laid out before us were burnt ruins of what used to be a grand hotel.

"No," Kelsey gasped.

A slag heap of burnt timbers and crumbled brick sat where the hotel used to be. I swallowed hard as my mind fought to figure out what to say, what to do next.

"No," Kelsey yelled as she ran towards the former building.

I rushed after her, desperate to ease some of her pain.

We slid to a stop in front of where the doors would have been and froze. Kelsey was lost and I felt useless. Did I hug her? Give her my support? Tell her everything would be okay.

Slowly the others came up behind us.

"She probably got out in time," Mrs. Carlson said.

Kelsey's chin dropped to her chest. "Even if she did, we'll never find her now."

"We need to find somewhere to spend the night. Somewhere safe," I said as I looked at the people in the park still staring at us.

Kelsey shot me an angry scowl. How dare I think about moving on?

I really don't know what would have happened. We could have spent the next two years searching. But just as I was preparing my arguments, a distant voice called out, "Kelsey!"

We all spun to see a woman running towards us, her hair whipping behind her. Dressed in jeans, a large gray hoody, and white tennis shoes, she looked like a soccer mom but the fear in her eyes made my stomach clenched.

"Mom!" Kelsey yelled and turned to run to her, both of them coming together in an epic hug.

I stood there and let them reconnect while keeping an eye on the people in the park. They were gathering, a group of men coming together. Some of them in suit jackets, others in jeans and leather jackets. Not a typical group, I thought. People thrown together by circumstances.

I would learn later they were mostly hotel guests and hotel workers with nowhere else to go.

"I can't believe it," Kelsey's mom kept saying as she would lean back, look at her daughter, then go back in for another hug.

Suddenly Kelsey broke away and said, "Mom, this is Ryan. Remember from across the street."

My gut tightened, there is something about meeting a girl's mom that just makes a guy nervous. This could go so wrong so fast. I'd almost rather face raiders trying to kill me than meet Kelsey's mom.

Mrs. Morgan stared at me for a long minute then smiled and reached out to pull me into a hug. "Thank you, thank you for giving me my daughter back."

I could only stand there and allow her to hug me. And yes, I admit, that was way better than being scowled at.

"Listen, we need to get out of here," I said as I glanced over my shoulder at the people gathering. I could see it, they were judging our level of weakness, gathering the determination.

Mrs. Morgan saw where I was looking and stiffened. "We need to go, John's got a place, they won't come after us there."

Okay, not what I expected, but I allowed her to lead the way.

"John?" Kelsey asked with obvious confusion.

Her mother blushed then said, "I'll explain later. Let's go. It's two blocks away."

A thousand questions danced through my head. Who was John? Where was his place? And would we survive the night? You know, just the basics.

Chapter Seventeen

Kelsey

Mom, I had found my mom. My mind still refused to believe it. I wrapped my arm around her waist, terrified she would disappear.

We hugged each other as she led us away from the ruined hotel and the people in the park. I quickly filled her in on our group, who, what, where, and why. I noticed Ryan slipping back to keep himself between us and the people in the park. Constantly glancing over my shoulder, I made sure he was keeping up.

Suddenly I was frightened I would lose him. A stomach gnawing fear. Just as I had found happiness it would surely be yanked out from beneath me. I mean, wasn't that what the world had turned into, constant disappointment and loss?

"I can't believe it," Mom said, over and over. "I came back every day."

"It was Ryan," I told her, "He saved us all, over and over."

She gave me a strange look, staring into my eyes, then smiled slightly and pulled us forward.

"We're going to his grandfather's farm," I told her. "In northern Idaho. All of us."

She frowned then glanced over at me with a strange look, my stomach tightened. She seemed different. Of course she was different. All of us had changed. The end of the world will do that to a person.

"This is Mrs. Carlson," I said then introduced the rest. She and Mrs. Carlson smiled at each other. That mom smile that said, what are you going to do? Isn't being a mom great?

A rush of adrenaline flashed through me as I babbled out our story. Escaping from Seattle. The earthquake, the tidal wave. The storms, the foul men at the Inn. The bodies hanging from telephone poles.

Mom just nodded, letting me get it all out.

"How? I mean, how did you survive?" I asked her.

She smiled weakly. "Someone let a candle catch a drape on fire. The sprinklers didn't work. The place was already becoming less than sanitary. A thousand guests, no working toilets. No food except what was in the room refrigerators. Someone raided the restaurant the second day.

"I made it out and was lost. I mean I didn't have anything but a robe. Bare feet. No Red Cross with blankets and hot cocoa. No firemen. Nothing. And my daughter was missing."

My heart ached.

"John found me," she said with a strange, almost ashamed look. "He got me to a safe place."

It hit me. Mom had been having her own adventures. It wasn't just Ryan and our group. But then it was happening to everyone at the same time. The sudden fight to survive. And so much of it chance. If Ryan hadn't seen me that morning. If he hadn't stopped, Mom would be alone. Never knowing I'd been washed away in a tsunami. If the kids had followed their teacher they'd be buried under a mountain.

Mr. Carlson dies trying to protect food for his family. Everything was so fragile, it sent a nervous flutter through my belly as I realized it would be like this forever.

"There," Mom said as she pointed across the street at a seedy Tavern. A dead neon sign said **102 Club**. Crammed between two larger brick buildings, One small frosted window. The place looked like somewhere a person went to become lost.

I stared at my mom, surprised, the woman I knew would never be caught dead in a place like this. I mean look at her. Jeans, tennis shoes, a hoody for god's sake. This wasn't my mom who preferred Versaci, Jacobs, or Louboutin. Even her hair was different, down, a headband. It was all just so strange.

She gave the others a quick smile then hurried across the street. I noticed she didn't look both ways. The habit was already broken. Roads weren't for cars anymore.

Knocking on the door, she stepped back, reaching out to take my hand. Shooting me a nervous smile.

I could hear three or four locks turning inside and then a heavy thud. Slowly, the door was cracked just enough for a shadow to peek out from the dark.

There was an angry grunt before the door was opened to reveal a middle-aged man in a stained T-shirt. A full beard starting to go gray, pot-bellied, and a neck tattoo of a penguin obviously done in prison, and oh yeah, a huge shotgun that he looked like he knew how to use instinctively.

"Hurry," Mom said as she ushered us inside glancing up the block to see if anyone was watching.

The man growled under his breath but backed up enough to wave us in with his shotgun.

I gawked at my first time inside a bar. A faint yellow light from two candles let me see a room full of tables and chairs and a long bar with stools. Behind the bar a shelf with two dozen bottles. A beer tap with three handles. Wow, it was impossible to imagine my mother being comfortable in this kind of place.

"This is my daughter," Mom said to him as she pulled me close. "I told you she'd come. Kelsey, this is John Perkins."

The man scowled at me then shot Mom an angry look and shook his head as he picked up the heavy metal bar used to block the door. "I said your daughter. Not a gaggle of geese."

My stomach tightened. So much for a warm welcome. As I looked around I caught a glance from Ryan and could read his mind. Where were the dangers? Was there another way out? Who was this man? He examined John and I could tell he wasn't impressed.

I introduced the others. Mrs. Carlson held all three of the kids, her back to the door, obviously terrified of being kicked out at the same time dreading being in the place. I felt it too, a nervousness. I couldn't put my finger on it, but I didn't want to be there.

"John saved me," Mom said as if that explained everything. "He brought me here."

"Best place," he said as he lifted a heavy bar and slid it into brackets to barricade the door. "Bar food, booze, what more do you need? Except for a pretty woman," he added as he reached an arm around my mom's waist and pulled her in tight before dropping his hand and squeezing her butt.

Mom blushed.

My jaw dropped when she didn't slap him, a small miracle in my view.

Ryan stiffened next to me. God! Again, I could feel that protectiveness just radiating off him. I swear he was going to get himself killed someday. Especially against a man like this.

"You have food?" Mrs. Carlson asked with a tremor in her voice. I noticed we were all ignoring his rudeness. I thought about the one pound of cornmeal and jar of olives we had and prayed we didn't have to dip into it.

John shot Mom a questioning look then let his shoulders slump. "Some," he said as he laid his shotgun on the bar then pulled out a large clear plastic container of Chex-mix. "We started with six of these. Down to the last two."

"And here," Mom added as he placed two oranges next to the container. My heart leaped as I wondered if this would be the last orange I ever ate.

"Want a beer?" John asked Ryan. "They're warm, but they're still beer."

Ryan declined then smiled and said, "I'm watching my weight," as he patted his stomach.

John frowned, not getting the joke then shrugged as he pulled out two cans of Reiner beer, downed the first in one long swallow then took a hefty sip of the second.

In the meantime, Mrs. Carlson had opened the Chex-mix then held it out, letting each of the kids grab a handful. Mom went behind the bar and returned with five Cokes and a Sprite. One for each, I realized as my insides melted, "Thank you."

Mom frowned as she watched us stuff our faces. I think she was beginning to understand what we had been through.

I swear, that food was like leveling up. Regaining our lost power. The sugar hit a person like a jolt and my body sighed with contentment.

"What's it been like?" Ryan asked John. As always, scoping out the terrain, looking for dangers, planning a way out. In other words, thinking about protecting us.

John frowned then shrugged. "A few crazies, Especially at night. Things are getting worse though. Those that got food are keeping it from those that want it."

Ryan glanced over at the door then peeked around the corner to look in the back and nodded when he saw the back door was barricaded.

"What are you going to do when the food runs out?" Ryan asked him.

Scoffing, John took a long pull on his beer then said, "Find more. Take what I need."

A cold shiver ran down my spine as I realized that if that meant taking someone else's then so be it.

"Mom," I said as I turned to her. "Ryan's grandfather has a farm up in the mountains. The cities are going to be a death camp."

Ryan coughed then said, "We have to leave in the morning. The sooner we get away from here the better."

John belched then said, "Good luck kid. But Becca and I'll take our chances here."

My stomach fell to the floor. First off, Becca? Since when? It had always been Rebecca. The next thought was to wonder how this idiot could even think my mom would stay with him.

I glanced over at her and felt my heart skip when I saw doubt in her eyes.

"Mom!" I gasped, "You can't think about staying."

She hesitated for a moment as John frowned at her then said, "She ain't got a choice. She's staying." Without warning, he grabbed her wrist and pulled her to him.

My jaw dropped for the second time that day. But when she tried to pull away he just tightened down and refused to let her go. Fear jumped her eyes. "John, I have to go with her."

He growled and clamped down even harder.

My anger was building to fight with my confusion. I was still trying to figure out what to do when Ryan solved the problem.

He pulled his pistol and pointed it at the man, then said, "Mrs. Morgan. You're coming with us unless you say otherwise."

There was a long pause as John grumbled deep in his throat while he stared pure hate at Ryan.

Mom turned to John and said, "I'm not letting my daughter out of my sight. And she's too in love to stay here without him."

I swear I didn't blush, but I also didn't object, I was too terrified to disrupt things. The wrong move and someone would end up dead, maybe my Mom. Maybe Ryan..

John's face turned purple as he stared down at her then pushed her aside and reached for the shotgun on the bar top.

"Don't," Ryan snapped as he stepped forward and placed the barrel against the side of John's head before he could get to the shotgun. "Please don't. But if you, I won't bury you. We'll leave you for the rats."

I could only stare at Ryan. He was so calm as if every word was the god's truth.

Jake growled, pulling at the leash in Ryan's other hand as he bared his teeth.

John twisted to look at Ryan from the corners of his eyes, reading him. Evaluating, would the kid pull the trigger? He was ignoring the threat from Jake, the boy in front of him was the true danger. After half of forever, I saw the truth hit John. He was a hair's breadth away from waking up dead. Swallowing, he slowly moved his hand away from the shotgun.

"Kelsey, get it," Ryan said, never taking his eyes off the man in front of him. "Mrs. Calson, get any food you can find."

"Hey," John said, "that's mine."

Ryan smiled, "Hey, consider it payment for bruising Mrs. Morgans' wrist. Besides, we're just taking what we need. Wasn't that your plan?"

Chapter Eighteen

Ryan

A burning anger flashed through me. When he'd grabbed Mrs. Morgan, all my frustration, all my fury erupted and it took every bit of self-control to not pull that trigger. I swear, my finger cramped, desperate to just put this man out of our misery.

This man was a waste of oxygen. Worse, a waste of food. He would add nothing to our world. Just take and destroy until someone stopped him.

I know, I know. Not very civilized. And two weeks earlier, impossible to believe. But things were different. I think it was the look of shock in Kelsey's eyes that stopped me from pulling that trigger.

Mrs. Carlson scrambled behind the bar, shooting me looks to make sure I wasn't going to go crazy. But, I've got to give her credit, she scrounged the two tubs of mix and a jar of cherries. She smiled sadly and held up a box of shotgun shells.

I nodded without taking my eyes off idiot. Mrs. Carlson backed out from behind the bar, making sure not to get between me and this idiot.

"Ryan," Mrs. Morgan sighed looking at me then at this John character. "He saved me. He didn't have to."

"Do you want to stay?" I asked her without taking my eyes off the man. I could see the pure hate in his eyes. I was taking what was his. The slightest waver and he'd be on me, taking my pistol and shoving it into places it wouldn't fit.

She sighed heavily then shook her head. "No."

John's eyes narrowed as he stared at her. "That wasn't what you said the other night, remember. You was screaming my name."

Mrs. Morgan's head dropped in shame but then she lifted it up and said, "I will always be thankful. But no, I don't want to stay with you."

I swear it was like watching a man get punched below the belt. A mixture of shock, hate, and pure pain.

"We need to go," I said as I handed Jake's leash to Tania. I wanted to be far enough away, find a place to hide before it got dark. I had planned on staying here, but I didn't think there were chains strong enough to keep this guy hog-tied for a night. There was too much rage.

When would we catch a break?

I made the others leave first then when I was sure they were out safe I said in my most serious voice, "I'm going to sit outside that door for a bit, waiting for you to come out. If it is in the next hour, I'm going to blow your head off. Mrs. Morgan and Kelsey will be far enough away so they won't see. Nobody will ever know and you'll just rot where you drop."

He stared back at me, trying to see if I was telling him the truth. I just stared back with my best poker face. I think the thing that helped was the realization that I was telling him the truth.

"I'll find you, kid. Some day. Some place. I'll kill you when you least expect it."

I laughed at him, "We'll probably all be dead next week, so get in line."

Backing out the door I pulled it closed behind me then stood there waiting. I swear I was going to shoot him if he came out.

Kelsey called from the corner. I paused giving him another minute then waved her to go on. I waited until they were all around the corner then backed away from the door. I kept it in sight until I reached the corner then ducked around it and rushed after my people. When I caught up to them I stashed the pistol in my waistband and held out my hand for the shotgun.

Kelsey handed it over like it was a hot potato and she couldn't get rid of it fast enough.

As we ran I kept looking over my shoulder expecting that monster to charge after us. Deep down, I couldn't really blame the guy, maybe his methods, but not his wants. He'd thought he'd found nirvana. A world without rules. A world where he could have a woman like Mrs. Morgan. A world where he was valuable.

And I'd just ruined his dreams.

"Tough Crap," I mumbled to myself as I kept myself between my people and the threat from behind.

We continued through town, up and down alleys, through a fast food joint that had been ransacked. Constantly moving, twisting, and turning, but putting distance between us and him.

It must have taken an hour or so before I noticed my people starting to drag, holding their sides, shooting me questioning looks.

"There," I said as I pointed to a gas station. I was looking for a place not already occupied. A place with enough windows to let in light. A place where we could hide and no one would think to look.

The place had been cleared out. Every candy bar, Slim Jim, and can of coke. The bare shelves a reminder of how the world had changed. The cash register had been shimmied open and emptied. I wanted to laugh. Paper money wasn't good for anything but the new toilet paper.

"Let's settle here," I said as I pointed to a back room. It had an emergency exit so we weren't trapping ourselves. I made sure they all got settled then went back out front where I could keep an eye on the roads. From my vantage point, I could see in three directions. Someone could get to me if they came in the back. But they'd only do that if they knew we were there.

Taking a deep breath, I tried to calm my racing heart. I had almost killed a man today. I mean, came really close. And I wasn't freaking out about it. What had happened to me?

The back room door opened and Kelsey came out, giving me a small smile. She hesitated for a moment then came to stand next to me as I slowly scanned out the window.

"Thank you," she said. "For saving my Mom."

I shrugged without taking my eyes off the roads. But God, her shampoo hit me like a sledgehammer upside the head. The bath at Mrs. Carlson's the night before had made me very aware of just how special a girl smells.

She looked down at her hands and my senses went on alert. I knew her now. More than I ever thought was possible. Two weeks of disasters will bring two people closer. That look meant she was worried, scared.

"What?" I asked her, trying to help her say what was bothering her.

She paused, then took a deep breath. "What my mom said. It was just her way of getting away from that man."

I scrunched up my eyebrows in confusion. "What did she say?"

Her eyes opened and I swear she didn't know whether to hit me or walk away. Finally, she said, "That part about knowing that I wouldn't stay because ..."

What was she talking about? I'd been so focused on the big idiot I hadn't been paying attention.

"... You know, about me being in love with you. That's why I wouldn't stay so she had to go. It was just words."

My gut tightened then I took a deep breath. "Kelsey. Don't worry about it. I'm not that dumb. Of course, I wouldn't think that she was serious. Besides, you guys barely had time to talk."

She looked at me with wide eyes, studying me, then she smiled just a bit before turning and looking out the window.

"Do you think he'll come after us? After her?"

Wow, that was a fast subject change. Okay, she was embarrassed. Obviously, the thought of Princess Kelsey ever being in love with me was ridiculous and she was embarrassed at the thought of anyone thinking that. It would totally ruin her status.

A sick feeling kicked around in the bottom of my stomach but I pushed it aside. We had bigger problems than my wounded pride.

"Maybe," I said. "But we could be anywhere. If we don't show ourselves. He won't have any clue."

She nodded. She was going to say something else but bit her tongue and just helped me keep an eye out. A sense of rightness filled me. Just having her there. Sharing this moment, helping me. The two of us standing against the world. It just felt right.

We spent the night in the gas station. Mrs. Carlson relieved me after a couple of hours, Then Mrs. Morgan took a turn. I just needed them to give me a warning if they saw anything while I grabbed a quick nap in the back.

Twice, Kelsey woke me that they saw someone but both times it turned out to be people looking for food. I just had to show myself and they took off.

The morning came bright and clear. The first clear day we'd had since this all started. It filled me with a small sense of hope. It is amazing how cloudy days can ruin a person's mood. Just knowing we weren't going to get rained on made the world seem better.

We had a handful of Chex-mix each and split an orange then hit the road. I worked us southeast until we hit I-90 again.

The shotgun felt heavy but I also felt a sense of power. Nobody messes with a 12-gauge pump shotgun. I offered my pistol to Mrs. Morgan who looked at me like I'd offered her a cobra. Mrs. Carlson however held out her hand.

"I don't know about them," she said. "But I can learn."

I gave her a five-minute lesson then kept us moving. We still peeked in every car or truck we passed but they were all empty. Although we did pick up a wool blanket for Mrs. Morgan. She and Kelsey walked next to each other, whispering, even laughing occasionally.

A smile creased my lips. Mrs. Morgan was still beautiful, Obviously, Kelsey would be a beautiful woman forever.

We were about a mile from the Idaho border when the first unease started tugging at my gut. People were walking towards Spokane, their heads dropping, angry. Others were gathered, more than any we had seen. Hundred. Families, individuals. Dressed in everything from suits to cut-off jeans. But a lot with blankets or rifles draped over shoulders.

"What's going on," Kelsey asked as she hurried to catch up next to me.

I just shrugged then asked an older woman, "What's going on?"

She frowned back at me and said, "They're not letting us in." The look of anger and fear in her eyes told me so much. This was a woman at the end of her rope. One more disappointment might push her over the edge.

My gut squeezed when I saw men in army camouflage with rifles blocking the bridge across the river and into Idaho. They'd pushed some vehicles together making an impregnable roadblock. Then my world took a dim turn when I recognized two 50 caliber machine guns poking out of some humvees, covering the crowd. Two grim-faced soldiers with their hands on the butterfly grips.

A rumble swept through the people, grumbles, curses, anger. I could see it so simply. They'd been moving towards this point, running away or running to. And here was something blocking their way.

I swear I could feel the tension building. The look on the soldiers' faces told me they could feel it too.

"Stay here," I told the others as I worked my way through the crowd. I'd almost reached the front when I felt someone take my hand. I looked and saw Kelsey smile up at me, silently asking to be included.

My gut told me to send her back where it was safer. But it felt just so wonderful to have her at my side.

When I got to the front, men were staring at the soldiers with hate. No one was yelling. That time had passed. Now they were just trying to figure out a way to break through.

Ignoring them, I made my way forward.

"Hold up," An officer yelled as he held up his hand to stop us.

I took a deep breath and asked, "How long is the road going to be closed."

The officer scowled and said, "As long as it takes. You people need to go home."

Laughing, I shook my head. "Our home was in Seattle. There's nothing to go back to."

He looked chagrined for a moment then shrugged, "Doesn't matter, you can't come in."

Scanning across the group of soldiers I examined them closely. National Guard would be my guess. Somehow they'd gotten enough to block the way into Idaho. Of course. They had food. Or at least enough for their population. But if Spokane's citizens poured into the state they'd be picked clean.

I thought about the men hanging from telephone polls in Cheney and shivered. These people weren't any different.

A sense of hopelessness filled me. We couldn't catch a break. I was about to argue with the officer when someone suddenly called my name, "Ryan? Ryan Conrad?"

I froze as a young soldier worked his way down the line to the officer and said something to him. The officer frowned and then nodded.

Smiling to myself I watched as Tim Devo worked his way through the cars and approached. He was dressed in camouflage like every other soldier and had a M-16 slung over his shoulder. I could only stare at him in disbelief.

"The last time I saw you," I said, "I was catching more trout than you."

He laughed, his eyes darting to Kelsey holding my hand then said, "Yeah, but I caught the biggest one."

Drawing close he stopped. We stared at each other for a long minute then came together in a bro hug, slapping each other on the back. Tim lived a few miles from my Grandfather. Or at least used to. Every summer he, Chase, and I would hang out, usually fishing, or hunting. Tim knew all the best spots.

I reached out and tugged at his uniform. "Since when?"

He laughed, "The smartest thing I ever did, joined the junior ROTC at the beginning of school. We all got drafted. But hey, at least they feed us."

Sighing inside I felt a sense of warmth. Here was a friend. Someone I had known before. A piece of my past.

Tim glanced over at Kelsey for like the sixth time then raised an eyebrow, obviously wanting an introduction. So, me, being me, I took her hand, subconsciously marking my territory. "This is Kelsey. We walked from Seattle. I've got to get to my Grandfathers."

Tim frowned and shook his head. "They won't let you in. And they're serious. We've got orders to shoot on sight."

The sadness in his eyes hit me. I wondered what had he been through. Maybe there were worse things than walking from Seattle. "How about up north?"

Shrugging he looked over his shoulder then leaned closer. "Maybe, Most of the Guard was pulled down here. It took us three days of marching. But they've got horse patrols all along the border."

My stomach fell. Kelsey looked like she'd just lost the state championship. We were trapped. My grandfather's farm was our hope. The one thing we could hold onto. The one way out of this misery.

Seeing her crushed feeling Tim took a deep breath. "If you did it at night. Maybe, way north. Find a logging road or a firebreak. You might make it. But ..."

I could only imagine how hard it would be. That was rough country up there. One of the many reasons Papa loved it.

"Thanks, Tim," I said as I patted his arm. "We've got to try. We don't have a choice."

He nodded then let out a long breath, "If you see my folks, tell them I'm doing fine. But I worry about them. They're all alone."

I nodded, I didn't tell him that we were all of us alone now.

"Devo," The officer yelled then motioned him back to the line.

Tim sighed heavily then said, "Don't take all the trout. Leave some for when I get back."

I laughed then felt a wave of sadness fill me as he turned and walked back to the barricade.

"Hey Tim," I yelled. He looked back over his shoulder. "Cassie is supposed to be coming up from Oklahoma. Chase from California, and Haley from New York. Dad warned them. Keep an eye out, Okay?"

He smiled and nodded.

Still holding Kelsey's hand I started leading her through the crowd. More than one person shot me angry glares. I had talked to the enemy. Was I one of them?

"We'll find somewhere to put up our tarp and stay here tonight. It's better being in a crowd."

"What then?" Kelsey asked

"He's right, if we do it smart we should be able to get through."

The doubt in her eyes pulled at me but like I had said earlier, we didn't have any choice.

Chapter Nineteen

Kelsey

My insides tumbled over themselves. Ryan held my hand as he wove us through the crowd. But he didn't drop it when we broke out the back side. It wasn't until he saw my mom staring at our clasped hands that he suddenly let it go like he'd been burned.

A sadness filled me. And it wasn't just being denied Idaho.

He pointed to a place off the road about fifty yards with some small trees where we could hang the tarp and set up camp.

"Do not break out the food where people can see it," he whispered as he looked around to make sure no one was listening.

"Why is everyone stopped?" Mom asked.

Ryan explained what was going on then said we'd move north and try and sneak in up there.

Mom turned and looked back at Spokane and I knew she was thinking about leaving John and having second thoughts. I know, not one of her best moments, but a woman does what a woman has to do. I told myself.

We had just gotten the tarp up and the blankets spread out. Ryan shook his head, "I'll sleep out here."

My heart lurched when I realized I wouldn't be able to cuddle up next to him tonight. It surprised me just how much I had become addicted to feeling his strength next to me. My next thought was to wonder if this was his way of detaching. Had Mom's words about me being in love with him scared him to his very toes?

Suddenly I was sure of it. An anger filled me at my Mom for ruining everything. How could she throw me under the bus like that? I mean, even if it was true, Ryan didn't need to know.

The sun was kissing the western horizon, a few fires had been started with families and groups centered around them. Suddenly, a commotion started at the border, people began hurrying, others rushing back to their camps and getting plates and bowls.

"Food," A guy called to us. "they're giving away food."

My stomach gurgled with hope. God, I had gotten so tired of that constant empty gnawing at my insides.

"Go," Ryan said. "I'll stay here and guard our stuff."

"I don't know," I pushed back.

"Hurry," he said with that exasperated look he gets when I'm being stupid, "Before it's all gone."

"Come on Kelsey," Mom said as Mrs. Carlson dug through the Rainbow Dash backpack for bowls.

The crowd buzzed with hope as we joined the line. The army had set up tables at the border with large kettles of soup and mounds of bread. They also had a dozen men with their rifles unslung. Ryan's friend, Tim, was one of them. He gave me a quick smile then glanced over at the food and relaxed when he realized there would be enough for us.

As we slowly inched forward in the line Mom turned to me and leaned down to whisper, "So Ryan? Have you slept with him?"

"Mom," I gasped as I frantically looked around to make sure no one had heard her craziness. "It's not like that. And I'm angry about you saying I'm in love with him."

She stared at me quizzically for a long moment then said, "You've got to be smart. This is not a time to get pregnant."

"Where you smart with John?" I snapped then immediately regretted it when the hurt hit her eyes. But she pulled herself together and said, "Yes, if you must know. But we're talking about you."

Grumbling under my breath I indicated she needed to move to keep in line.

"So Ryan?" she asked again, refusing to let the matter drop.

I rolled my eyes and ground my teeth. "He's a good person. And he doesn't think about me like that."

Mom laughed, "Oh honey, Ryan Conrad is a red-blooded boy. And you're a beautiful girl. Believe me, he thinks about you like that."

"Not all boys are monsters, Mom," I growled. I truly believe her bad luck with men had shaped her views.

She shook her head, "I'm not saying he is. He saved my little girl, he's a hero in my books. But, I just want you to be aware. You know."

I stopped inching forward and turned her so we were face to face, "Think about it, Mom. Really think about it. Do you believe there is someone better in this world? I mean really. The guy is smart, strong, supper brave, and taking us to a place where we can survive. And oh yeah, he's cute too."

She stared back at me, obviously surprised I was so adamant.

"It's not like I'm going to college," I said. "I'm not going to marry some doctor. Some Amazon bigwig. Can you really think there is anyone better than Ryan Conrad in this new world? Or the old world for that matter. I swear it's like he was designed to survive the worst they throw at him. I mean, you learned that with John. You saw the first big bad guy and latched on to him. The difference is that Ryan would never hurt me. And he'd never try to make me stay against my wishes. He's too good for that."

Mom didn't turn red, didn't start yelling, or give me the evil eye. She simply examined me for a moment then smiled widely. "For a girl not in love, You sure are protective."

My stomach fell as I realized that she could see right through me. She now knew perfectly well that I was madly in love with Ryan. And my worst fear was her trying to come between us, or worse, acting as matchmaker.

I just needed her to mind her own business. I didn't want anyone screwing this up.

Clenching my jaw I shut up, the sooner we stopped talking about it the sooner we could pretend none of it was true. Luckily it was our turn. Mrs. Carlson led our group through first. One ladle of potato soup and a slice of bread each.

I noticed Tim Devo catch the server's eye and nod at him. The server smiled at Mrs. Carlson and fished around until he had more potatoes than normal and gently plopped the soup in her bowl.

He did the same for each of us. The next server handed each person a slice of fresh bread. I swear he made sure to give us the larger pieces. I gave Tim a grateful smile. He smiled back, sighing, obviously pleased that he'd done at least one good thing that day.

We returned to camp to find Ryan had made a small fire. The day had turned to gray evening as we all carefully sat down, making sure to not spill any of our soup. Each of us broke off a small piece of bread, dipped it, then fed it to Jake.

Ryan smiled at us, obviously pleased before going to join the line.

Mom watched him walk into the growing night then shot me a knowing smile. I could read her mind. A handsome man.

I ignored her and focused on my meal. God, it was good. I don't know who the cook was but I would thank him for the rest of my life. A hot meal, seasoned just right. Either that, or I'd have enjoyed shoe leatheer if it had been cooked long enough.

As we ate, Paul passed the water bottle around then filled an empty bowl for Jake to drink from. We discussed why the Army had shut down the border and how far would we have to walk before we could sneak across.

I knew each of us where thinking about what would happen if they caught us. Just how serious were they?

The first star had peaked out and the moon was coming up when Ryan returned with a sad expression and a shrug of his shoulders.

"They ran out." I gasped as an anger flared inside of me. I then held out my slice of bread. I'd held it back just in case.

He didn't fight me on it. Didn't shake me off and deny that he needed it. I think we were past those silly games. He accepted it and said thanks. My heart soared. I liked that he accepted my help. It made me feel valued like I was worth something. But most of all, it gave me a sense of agency. Like I was in control of my life. At least a little part.

Later, as the fire died down, we worked our way in under the tarp. Mom taking the place where Ryan normally slept. She put her arm around me and I swear I cursed myself for feeling a twinge of regret.

My Mom was alive. We were reunited. I should have sunk into her embrace and just let her hold me. But a small part of me had moved on somehow. I mean. I had survived without her for two weeks.

Besides, I wished it was Ryan holding me. But, hey, I'm not perfect. Sometimes I know what I'm supposed to feel. But I don't always follow what I'm supposed to do. One of my many failings.

The next morning after a half handful of Chex-mix we hit the road. Leaving I-90 and working our way north. Several people saw us leave. Some scrunched up their eyebrows wondering where we were going. Others looked relieved, less competition for the next batch of food.

I think a group was going to ask to go with us, A man and three kids. But he sighed heavily and stepped back.

We crossed down a slope to a residential suburb. Not much different than the one around Mrs. Carlson's house back in Cheney. Only this one didn't have bodies hanging from telephone poles.

"Stay in the middle of the street," Ryan told us as he took the lead then nodded for Paul to fall back as sheepdog.

We worked our way through the housing development. Occasionally people would pull their curtains back. Twice men stepped out of their front door, always heavily armed. Obviously letting us know they weren't an easy target.

Ryan would just nod in their direction. Silently telling them we were no threat and we would keep moving.

We'd almost made it out of the houses when a blood-curdling scream hit us from a house on the right. The kind filled with madness and pure pain.

"Go," Ryan said, waving us forward.

My heart fell. No investigating, no helping other people. His first goal was to get us away from any danger.

Suddenly a shot rang out from inside the house and the screams stopped, putting a pawl over the entire neighborhood. An eerie silence that just punctuated how screwed up this new world was.

After the houses, we found a road headed due north as we slowly moved into forest and small homesteads.

"Should we try and find an empty place," Mrs. Carlson called. "Or somewhere they might take us in."

Ryan shot me a knowing look then shook his head. "Anywhere we stop might be a place other people will want also. And no one will want to help us. Not if they're smart."

I thought of that awful scream. He was right. We were on our own. And yes, if we found the perfect empty house. Either it would already have squatters or it would be a target for the next people to come along.

Instead, later that afternoon we found a place next to a large lake, back off the road where a fire wouldn't be seen.

"Wait until dark before we start a fire," he said then grabbed the fishing line and hooks and started for the lake.

Mom gave me a puzzled frown.

"People won't see the smoke," I told her, sort of proud of myself.

We got busy setting up camp and gathering wood for the night. I kept looking towards where Ryan had disappeared, worried. I didn't like him being out of sight. Too many things could go wrong.

Shaking my head at myself I couldn't help but smile. Who would ever have imagined I would worry about where Ryan Conrad might be and what he was doing? I know I couldn't have imagined it.

Suddenly, I needed to do something for him. A need deep inside of me at the instinctive level. It took me a minute to figure out what. I used my pocket knife to cut an armful of ferns and laid them out as a bed a foot thick then draped his blanket over them.

Would he be pleased? God, I was worried he wouldn't see what I had done for him. Either that or think I was a silly girl who didn't know he preferred sleeping on the hard ground.

As we waited, Paul pulled out the last plastic container of Chex-Mix. I told him to hold off until Ryan came back. "He might have dinner."

Paul nodded and put the container back. Mom gave me a strange look.

"What?" I asked her. She simply smiled and shook her head then said. "You lot don't need Mrs. Carlson or me."

I could only stare as I realized she was right. In only two weeks we'd gotten past the need for adults. In fact, we had moved into their level. Maybe even a bit more. We could adapt faster I think. We weren't so tied to the old world. I would miss it, but I could get past it. I worried about people like Mrs. Carlson and Mom. Would they always be looking back? Looking at what they had lost instead of figuring out what they had to do to get what they needed.

But before I could think about it too much, Ryan came back, holding up three pounds of fish. A smile a mile wide on his face, thrilled we would eat tonight.

As he came into camp he caught sight of the mound of ferns and his blanket. He immediately shot me a look then smiled.

My heart soared, one, he knew instinctively that I was the one to make it for him. Two, because he was pleased. And three, because his smile churned up a feeling of pure happiness deep in my soul.

Chapter Twenty

Ryan

My stomach was at that in-between point. We hadn't been starving long enough for it to go numb. Every day was that driving need to find food. My mind had become more focused than ever as I constantly tried to solve our problem.

It was strange. Before, food had never been an issue. I mean never. There was always something in the house. More than enough. And if we were away from the house, there were a thousand places to get food.

Now. It had all disappeared. People were hoovering up everything they could find, or hoarding what they had. The thing is, I knew there was food out there. Last year's crop still In silos, cattle on ranches, and warehouses full of canned goods. But there was no way to get that food to where the people were.

Our entire system had been designed to move the food from where it was produced to where the people lived. I remembered my Papa telling me that back in the eighteen hundreds, ninety percent of the people were involved in growing food. Then they invented the combustible engine. People moved off small farms to the cities.

A hundred years or so of advancement and plenty until a rock from space threw us back. We just weren't set up to live in this new world. Not at these numbers.

Cursing, I spit into the dirt thinking about the army keeping us from even trying.

The morning had turned cloudy again. I wondered if I'd be rained on later. I needed to stop early enough to build a lean-to for Jake and myself.

I glanced over my shoulder to make sure people were keeping up. We'd moved into forests and foothills with the occasional farm then came out along the Pend River which made me sigh inside. Hopefully, I could get enough fish to keep us going.

As we walked I kept a lookout for anything we could use. I found a chunk of baling wire next to the road and spent the day working it into snares as I walked.

That night, I got us off the road and over a small ridge before we settled in. While the others made camp I set the snares and then hit the river but got skunked. It was flooding and too fast.

The look of disappointment in everyone's eyes was like a kick to the gut.

We munched on the last of the Chex-mix and I saw more than one of them glancing at the empty jar with fear. What would we eat tomorrow? That had become the constant thought at the front of our brains.

As I lay under the lean-to I glanced over at the group scrunched up together under the tarp and felt a little lost. I missed holding Kelsey at night. At the same time, a guilty feeling of failure continually ate at my gut.

They were hungry. People were getting lean. Too lean in my eyes. The ten to twenty miles of walking every day, the missing calories. We couldn't keep this up, I realized. We'd tire out before we got to Papa's

If I could just get them there. He'd have food. I mean, he put up enough every year to feed a family of four for a year. Only, ever since Nanna died ten years ago, and his two sons had left. He never went through all the food and just kept adding to it. He'd have years worth.

My stomach cramped with need as I thought about sauerkraut and dried apples.

We were maybe twenty miles from where I wanted to cross over when we got lucky. I mean, real lucky. A small group of Canadian geese skimmed down low looking to land on a pond. Without thinking, I unslung the shotgun and fired. A bird dropped, bouncing when it fell. I was lucky, buckshot mangled a bird, but we weren't going to turn it down.

We feasted that night, picking the bird clean. I sat back and felt a sense of satisfaction. I had fed my tribe. We would survive another day.

Kelsey suddenly got up from the log she was sitting on and came over to sit next to me. She gave me a warm smile and sighed. "Thank you."

I shrugged. Soaking up her warm scent. She'd washed her hands with our only bar of Irish Spring bar soap that morning. Her hair was pulled back in a ponytail. She looked different I realized. Yes, leaner, but there was more. Something in her eyes that made her look older, wiser, and somehow even more beautiful. She'd lost that pampered princess look and replaced it with competent woman, trusted friend look.

I know, not flattering. Not what a girl wants to hear. But it was true and my heart ached with a need to just hold her. Smartly, I refrained from making an idiot of myself and just nudged her with my shoulder and said. "You wait, when we get there, we'll eat three times a day. You'll see."

She smiled and said, "I remember ordering a salad at McDonald's because I was worried about gaining weight. It seems so silly. God, what I wouldn't give for a Big Mac.

I could only nod as I stared into the fire, simply enjoying sitting next to her. I glanced over and saw her mom looking at us with a secret smile. A nervousness filled me. If her mom knew the thoughts I had about her daughter she'd gut me and nail my pelt to a barn door.

The full stomachs didn't last. I failed to find food the next day and we went to bed that night hungry. A gut-gnawing hunger that put fear in everyone's eyes.

"How much further?" Kelsey asked as she sat down next to me.

I glanced over at the tarp. The others had gone to bed. Mrs. Carlson was snoring. Jake and I had sat up a little longer, me feeding the fire small sticks as I dreaded the next few days. We needed food.

"We'll find a logging road or fire break headed east tomorrow and start across," I told her.

"What if they try to stop us?"

I knew what she really wanted to know. Did I think they would really shoot us if we tried?

Shrugging, I said, "They can't be everywhere. That's rough country."

A nervousness filled me as I tried to anticipate all the things that could go wrong. Ways around possible scenarios, but deep in my heart I knew no matter how much I planned, we'd just have to figure it out as we went along.

Suddenly, Kelsey hugged me and kissed me on the cheek. "You'll figure it out."

I stared, unable to believe what had just happened. I stared into her eyes, trying to understand this new dynamic, this girl. She didn't look away. Her arms didn't drop from my shoulder.

We looked into each other's eyes for half of forever before I realized what needed to happen. Without thinking, I leaned forward and took her lips with mine.

The girl didn't back away. She didn't gasp and slap me. Instead, she sank into that kiss like she'd wanted it forever.

My world changed at that moment. I know. A silly expression. But it was so true. My feelings for Kelsey didn't change. But the feelings about myself changed. She liked me. She wanted me to kiss her. It made me feel like I could move mountains. A burning need to protect her filled my soul. Nothing in this world was allowed to ever hurt her.

We kissed, then sighed and laid our foreheads against each other, both gasping for breath, both enjoying the moment.

She sighed heavily then took a deep breath. I froze, waiting for her to say something like she was wrong. Or that we should only be friends. But instead, she sighed again and snuggled down next to me, laying her head on my shoulder.

I wrapped an arm around her shoulders and allowed myself to just be. To accept this new thing. Yes, we didn't talk about our feelings. Didn't share what we felt. But we didn't need to. At least I thought so.

Of course, that led to a thousand thoughts. Was I misreading that kiss? The look in her eyes? Maybe she didn't feel what I felt. We should talk about it. But I kept myself locked up. No way was I saying anything. Either this was the most perfect thing in the history of the world. Or it wasn't. In which case, I didn't want to know.

A cool breeze came in from the north making her shiver. I threw another log onto the fire then reached over and snaked my blanket out from my lean-to and draped it over our knees and pulled it up to her chin.

She shot me a quick smile. No words. But a look that made me know everything was as it should be.

Snuggling down under the blanket she took my hand in both of hers and sighed. I squeezed her shoulder letting her know I agreed.

We woke the next morning still holding hands. I glanced down at her. She smiled as her cheeks blushed with the cutest embarrassment.

"Morning Princess," I said.

"Only you are allowed to call me that."

I laughed then nudged her. I needed to get up and get moving. My body was stiff in so many ways.

Mrs. Morgan lifted up and saw us sitting next to each other and frowned. I don't think she was happy about it. But who could blame her? She'd just lost her daughter to a strange boy she barely knew.

With no breakfast, it didn't take long to get started and we were soon on the road. The foothills had become mountains. It was up and over ridges, down into small valleys then climbing again.

Finally, I found what I wanted. A logging road headed east. I stopped everyone and examined it. I was pretty sure it'd been cut in a year or two earlier to clear-cut a section up on the hill to the east.

Turning back to everyone I said, "We need to cross over the border if we're going to get there. I figure this is the best place. When we get to where I think the border is, we'll find a trail and work our way through the forest. About two or three miles."

The others looked.

"Do you think we can find food along the way?" Paul asked. He'd been hit hard. A growing boy that age burns through calories like a steam engine.

"I doubt it," I said with sadness. "And keep it quiet. Sound travels farther than you think."

Kelsey reached out and took my hand. "Well eat when we get there. Two or three days."

A look of pure panic flashed through them. Three days of no food after all they had been through. Their bodies were screaming for nurishment and now they had to wait another three days. It might be impossible.

I squeezed her hand then nodded to the road, telling Paul to bring up the rear. Tania dropped back to walk with him. I could see it in their eyes, the hunger, the tiredness, the beginning of the loss of hope.

Mrs. Carlson would glance at her children with sad eyes. My soul hurt at the thought of watching your children starve. Knowing the pain eating them up inside and being unable to feed them. It went against every atom of a mother's heart.

Kelsey's mom pulled Kelsey aside and whispered something. Kelsy just smiled then shrugged.

We really needed to talk I thought. But at the moment, I needed to get them across.

The logging road had just been scraped into the soil and was just wide enough for a logging truck to get down from the hills above us. All of the rains had turned it muddy but it had dried out enough along the sides. I couldn't imagine getting up this road a week earlier.

As we approached where I thought the border might be my head constantly shifted, scanning, my ears listening. Would they really shoot us? Why? I mean we were women and kids mostly.

It felt impossible. This was America. We didn't do stuff like that. But deep down, there was enough doubt that I didn't want to press the point.

I was just beginning to think we'd make it when I spotted horse droppings in the middle of the dirt road. Fresh, I realized, Hay fed, with shod hoof prints. Holding up a hand to stop everyone behind me I examined the area.

A person had stopped there a couple of hours ago would be my guess. Stopped and scanned the area. Down the road, across a clear cut. They knew this was a good spot to cross.

"That way," I hissed as I pointed to the closest tree line. I needed to get them out of sight. Without checking to make sure they were following, I started racing across the clear-cut, jumping over stumps and brambles.

Please, I begged as my shoulders hunched, expecting a bullet at any moment.

When we made the trees we collapsed, gasping for breath. No one had any energy anymore. The smallest thing seemed to take it out of us.

As we gathered our breath I was trying to work out our next step when everyone froze. Three men were riding down the road, two in front, one behind, all in camo, all with rifles out and ready for use.

"Damn," I cursed. If they saw our footprints it'd be like a neon sign pointing to us. Seven people can't move across a field without leaving a trail a mile wide.

"Go," I whispered as I got them hurrying deeper into the forest. I gave the men one last look then scurried after my people. Working my way to the front I kept them going, Down a bank to a small creek, across and up over a ridge. Always keeping them in the trees.

We topped out over the second ridge then slid down the pine needles to the bottom. Paul tripped and grabbed his ankle but bounced up and shook his head at me. He could keep going. Limping, but moving.

"This way," I said as I followed the dry bed between ridges. Several times the walls closed in tight. Too tight for a horse, I thought with a smile. We just needed to get away and they'd never find us.

We'd been running for almost an hour when Julia collapsed, holding her side, gasping for breath. Everyone else bent over fighting to breathe.

"Stay here," I said, which was sort of redundant, no one was moving no matter what.

Making sure they understood, I headed back up the ridge we'd just crossed. I needed to know we were safe. If not, I'd push them along if I had to kick them in the butt. Either that or carry them. My people weren't getting shot. Not on my watch.

Chapter Twenty-One

Kelsey

I forced myself to stand straighter so I could watch Ryan scramble back up the hill we'd just come down.

My heart ached. What if something happened to him? I hadn't told him how I felt. The thought of him dying without knowing hurt my very soul. God, what an idiot I'd been. I mean, we could have been spending all this time knowing the truth. Sharing. Two people together instead of two individuals walking next to each other.

Taking a deep breath I was about to start following him when Mom grabbed my arm. "He said to stay here."

"But."

"No,"

I stopped and looked at her. This was my mother. I'd always done what she told me. At least while she was there watching. But something had changed last night. My priorities. My loyalties were different.

No, Ryan might need me, I shrugged off her hand and started back up the hill. She gasped and I saw a look of lost pain in her eyes as she realized her little girl wasn't hers anymore.

Using my hands, I tried to pull myself up the hill, grabbing tree trunks as my feet slipped on the pine needles. I made it almost halfway up when Ryan met me coming down. His brow furrowed in confusion before he shook his head.

"You don't listen, do you?"

My cheeks grew warm with embarrassment. "Someone has to make sure you know what you're doing."

The words had no sooner left my mouth than I wanted to pull them back. He might think I was criticizing him. I mean, the guy was a God when it came to survival.

The small smile and twinkle in his eyes made me relax. He knew I was teasing. Wow, why was Ryan so different? Any other boy I knew would have that whole male ego thing going full blast and never have seen my lame attempt at humor. Not Ryan. Why? Was it him? Or did he just get me?

Or was it two weeks of stress and terror that brought us onto the same wavelength? I thought about what Mom said a few days back. Would Ryan and I have had anything in the old world? I honestly don't know.

Maybe it took something like this to change people enough to where they could see the hidden truth about each other.

We hadn't talked about last night. But that kiss sort of said everything that needed to be said. I mean, I'd kissed boys before. But no kiss had ever been like that. A toe-curling blockbuster of a kiss.

The kind a girl remembers for the rest of her life. But there had been more. The kindness in his eyes when he looked at me. The squeeze of his arm around my shoulder just to let me know everything was perfect.

But it had been a simple acceptance. No need to talk about it. The kiss and all the feelings just felt too natural to be talked about. All because Ryan felt towards me like I felt towards him. I mean. Is there anything more perfect?

A feeling of being accepted filled me, making me want to hug him and hold onto him forever. But he slid past me and down to the others.

"I think we lost them," he said. Smiles broke out as people slumped down to sit on the hard ground, grateful they didn't have to keep running.

"We need to find water and a place to camp," Ryan said then told Paul to lead the way.

Everyone sighed heavily as they pushed themselves to stand and started up the cut between the ridges. I noticed that Ryan fell back, constantly looking over his shoulder. As always, he kept himself between us and any danger.

It didn't take long before Paul found a puddle deep enough to get water.

"We'll boil it tonight," Ryan said as he looked around and pointed to where he wanted the tarp set up. "I'll set some snares. Maybe I'll get lucky."

Again he left us, scrambling up the far ridge. God, did the boy ever rest. Where did he find the energy? I felt like a wrung-out dish rag. It took a force of will to make my body move and help set up the tarp.

Once things were set up and the fire laid, we sat down, waiting for dark. Ryan slid down the hill on his butt and sat down next to me.

Julia shot me a strange look but I ignored her. I'd won. There was no need to rub her nose in it. Besides, I was more interested in snuggling in next to him and just enjoying my life.

No one talked, we just looked at nothing and tried to ignore the gnawing pain in our stomachs. Paul fiddled with a stick, making marks in the ground, his jaw set, struggling to not fight or yell.

Mom and Mrs. Carlson both looked wiped out, their hair knotted, Mrs. Carlson's jacket had been ripped at the shoulder, exposing the padding. Tania sat next to Paul, her eyes watching him draw in the dirt then she suddenly reached over, took the stick from his

255

hand, and drew a tic-tac-toe matrix in the dirt, marked an X then handed him the stick.

Julia scowled at her brother then leaned on her mother.

I shifted and felt my leg cramp as if someone had put it in a bench vice.

"OOOW," I hissed as I grabbed my calf.

Both Mom and Ryan moved to help me. And luckily, Ryan was closer. Shooting me a concerned smile he started rubbing my cramping leg as I fought to get it into just the right position.

"No vitamins," he said as he used both hands on the leg. My mind of course was more focused on the pain than the fact that the boy I loved was massaging my leg. I know, not my best moment.

When he rubbed the cramp out and I was able to stretch out he glanced down at the ground and sighed heavily. I knew him. He was hurting because I was hurting.

The seven of us sat around the fireless fire until it got dark enough. Ryan finally used his lighter to start the fire then filled our two biggest pots to boil the water, keeping them at a running boil for ten minutes at least then gingerly set them aside to cool.

"It's late," Mrs. Carlson said with a heavy sigh and motioned for her children to go to bed. I sat, refusing to move from Ryan's side.

After they settled in, Jake got up and joined them, curling in next to Paul.

"I think he knows I want to be alone with you," Ryan whispered in my ear.

"I always knew he was a smart dog."

The firelight danced, catching his smile and making my insides melt. "Do you want to go for a walk?" he asked with just a hint of trepidation that was cuter than anything ever. "It might help with the cramp."

All I could do was nod. Like I said, melted heart.

He held out a hand and helped me up then led me back down the cut around a bend. Just before we disappeared I looked back and saw Mom rise up and give me a concerned look. God, you'd think I was being kidnapped by a dozen bikers. This was Ryan Conrad. Nothing was going to happen unless I wanted it to.

It was dark, the clouds never went away, but our eyes had adjusted enough to see our way.

My heart pounded in my chest the further we got away. A combination of hope and fear all mixed in with the just pure tension. The good kind. The kind that keeps a girl up at night. A need that I was just then beginning to come to grips with.

"Here," Ryan said as he pointed to a little bench cut into the ridge by erosion.

I sighed inside as I sat, suddenly very nervous and very excited. We were alone. For the first time in forever.

Ryan sat down next to me and took a deep breath. "Um … Kelsey," he began.

I turned to face him then threw myself on him, unable not to.

I won't talk about that night. There are some things too special to be spoken about. It would almost be sacrilege to share it with you. If you know what I mean. If you don't, I am sorry. Every person should experience a night like that once in their life.

The moon came out just before it set when Ryan led me back into the camp and whispered I should go join the others. He would stay up feeding the fire.

I glanced over at him and couldn't stop from smiling. I swear I didn't think I would ever be able to not smile again. My heart was full of the wonders of the world. He smiled back and I knew I would love this man for the rest of my life.

Yes, we might die tomorrow. But it would be as a woman in love with a good man. A man who loved her. You've got to admit, it is more than most people have in this screwed-up world.

I shook my head and whispered, "I'll stay, we can take turns napping."

He smiled, obviously pleased, which made my heart pound even harder. He didn't want to toss me aside.

The next morning we started working east, staying off logging roads or firebreaks. Northern Idaho is rough and sparsely populated. I mean no roads, no backwoods cabins. Not even popular trails full of tourist hikers. Just ridge after ridge.

Working our way through the forest it took us almost all day to make maybe five miles. Every time we crested a ridge I'd look over at Ryan silently begging him to tell us we were there. But he'd take a deep sigh then start down.

When we came across a logging road he'd stop and have us hunker down while he scoped it out then wave us across like we were an invading army. We'd rush across, hunched over, terrified of being spotted then slip into the trees and feel safe.

As we worked our way along a creek, Ryan suddenly hissed, "Yes,"

I froze then hurried up to him, "What."

He smiled widely and pointed, "Cattail. Roots."

A clump of cattails, hundred of them filled a marshy spur of the creek. Without saying anything, Ryan pulled his knife and waded into the water up to his knees and started digging, throwing the long spindly roots onto the bank on the other side of the creek.

The rest of us watched, fighting internally at the disgusting thought of eating weird plants and gurgling stomachs demanding to be fed.

Once he had about twenty pounds, he started cutting spring shoots and tossed them in with the rest. Shivering from the cold water, he stepped out and showed us what to do. We all pitched in, cutting off the small off-shoots from the roots. Washed them, then set them aside. That dropped it down to about ten pounds.

Ryan's hands were bright red and he couldn't stop shivering. A mountain stream in early spring will sap the warmth out of a person faster than a freezer set on high. Especially when they had already burned off any fuel

"Go change," I told him. I know, demanding girlfriend. I didn't ask, I ordered and felt my insides tighten, suddenly terrified he'd be mad at me.

This was why we needed to talk, I realized. We needed to define exactly what this was. I needed to know my boundaries. Holding my breath I waited.

Ryan of course simply grabbed his spare clothes and walked off to change. Mom shot me a look that I couldn't understand. I ignored her and returned to help clean the cattail roots.

"We'll boil them," he said as he walked back, tucking his shirt in, "And sauté the spring shoots. They sort of taste like cucumber. But they'll fill our stomachs. It'd be nice if we could find some wild onions, but we're out of luck."

The meal that night wasn't the most appetizing, but he was right, our bellies were full. The roots tasted like a granular potato on the green side. If you know what I mean. They just needed, salt, pepper, a pound of butter, and a steak, and they'd be acceptable. But like I said, they filled our stomachs.

That night, while we sat next to each other, our backs to a log, Jake came over and sat down next to me, laying on my leg. I started to ruffle his neck as I realized he did that, going to different people at different times, sharing himself.

"How much further?" I asked Ryan as I continued to pet Jake.

Ryan shifted to get out of the drifting smoke then said, "We'll be there tomorrow."

"What?" I gasped.

"Yeah, maybe five miles. I think we should see the road from the next ridge. Work our way down, cross, then find my Papa's"

I took a deep breath as I realized our journey was coming to an end. Would things change between us? What if his grandfather didn't like me? Or any of us? What if he didn't want to take us in?

Six strangers was a lot to take on. I don't care what Ryan said, most people would not be pleased.

"What if your grandfather doesn't want us."

Ryan's brow furrowed then he laughed, "Your family. He doesn't have a choice."

My heart melted. It seemed to do that a lot around Ryan. I leaned my head on his shoulder and decided I'd just trust him. Tomorrow night I would be sleeping inside a warm home. I'd sit down at a table and eat a regular meal.

Oh, how wrong can a girl be?

Chapter Twenty-Two

Ryan

I found a deer trail and used it to work our way around the next ridge. Reaching out, I helped Kelsey up and over a huge log across the trail. She shot me a quick smile then squeezed my hand. Okay, I'll admit it and acknowledge she had me wrapped around her little finger. I would have done anything just to see that smile.

The previous night had changed me, made me want so much more. Focus on her like a laser beam. Careful, Ryan, I told myself. Do not become one of those hovering, possessive boyfriends. But, I just couldn't get her out of my mind.

I mean the girl was beyond beautiful. Yes, an angel's face, and a body that called to my soul. But she was so much more. Funny, kind, smart, and, peaceful. If that makes any sense. I mean, in the last two weeks. She hadn't created drama. Heaven knows, there was more than enough drama. But it wasn't Kelsey's doing.

Don't get me wrong. She wasn't a pushover. She couldn't have gone through all this if she was. Suddenly I realized it was because she wasn't self-centered. I know, blowing up all my preconceived biases about cheerleaders.

I gave her a smile then reluctantly let go of her hand so I could move up to the front. The trail weaved its way between trees. The air smelled of pine and moldy leaves. A hundred hunting and fishing trips danced through my mind. All of them associated with that smell.

Bending at the waist, I worked my way up a slope then froze. There on the trail, the perfect print of a mountain lion. A big one. Fresh.

Unslinging my shotgun, I held up my hand to stop the others as I scanned the forest. God, the beast could be anywhere I realized. Four feet away, ready to pounce, and I wouldn't be able to see it.

"Jake," I called as I tapped my leg. Tania unclipped his leash and let him come to me.

He immediately started sniffing the print. And I swear he got a gleam in his eye at the smell of cat.

"Careful," I told him. "This isn't some house tabby."

He snuffed, obviously disagreeing. Cat was cat. Arch enemy. He immediately started hurrying up the trail, his nose to the ground. I waved everyone forward then followed my dog, trusting that he would give me warning.

Jake suddenly barked and darted into the trees.

"No!" I yelled as my heart dropped. He was going to get ripped to shreds. I just knew it.

"JAKE" I called in my commanding voice. He was trained. I mean really well trained. But his instincts to protect had taken over.

"JAKE," I growled. "COME, NOW."

Cursing under my breath I was about to follow him into the bushes when he popped out a dozen feet ahead on the trail, his tail wagging a mile a minute. Telling me he had chased off the threat. And why had I called him back? He could have finished it off, no problem. Besides, he seemed to say. You haven't been feeding me, so I'll just get my own.

I could only shake my head then tell Tania to clip his leash on. Shaking my head, I pushed us up the trail then cut into the trees to get to the top of the ridge. When I crested out I froze and knew my forehead was creased in confusion.

"What?" Kelsey asked as she came to stand next to me and looked down at the two-lane rural road below us.

"That doesn't belong there," I said pointing down at a gravel quarry. "Or we don't belong here."

"We're lost?" she gasped.

"Not lost so much," I replied as I tried to get my bearings. "I'm pretty sure we're in

266

Idaho still. I don't think we've crossed over into Montana."

Her eyebrows shot up as the color drained from her face. I could read it so easily. If you don't know for sure what state you're in. You're pretty much lost.

My gut turned over as I frantically tried to work it out. "We must have come out too far north. I haven't spent much time up here, north of his farm."

"How far?" she asked, holding her breath.

"A couple of miles, I bet."

Her shoulders slumped with relief. "I thought you were going to say another twenty, four more days. I've got to be honest. I am tired of walking up and down mountains."

I had to smile and sighed with relief as I motioned everyone to stay on the back side of the ridge and worked our way south. Every so often I'd go up on top and look over, searching for any landmark.

It took us an hour before I spotted a bend in the road and knew where we were at.

We hunkered down just behind the ridge and finished the last of the cattail roots. "We need to cross the road then go about a mile south to catch my grandfather's dirt road to his house."

They looked back at me with blank emptiness. I could see it in their eyes. They were done. I'd pushed them too hard for too long. My insides clenched up in a ball as I felt a wave of guilt. But I was going to have to push them again. But they looked so ... Bedraggled, was the word. Cuts and bruises, torn clothes, dirty faces. And that god-awful blank stare.

"It's all downhill from here," I said as I gave them a smile. "Crossing the road won't be dangerous. No vehicles and I can see a long distance, no horsemen."

Kelsey stood up, dusting off the back of her pants, and shot me a quick smile of support. The others grumbled and moaned but they got up, collectively taking a deep breath for that last push.

When I got to the ridge top I held up for a minute and checked it out. The thought of getting caught the last mile ate at my gut. Coming all this way only to end up either lined up and shot or worse, hanging from a telephone pole. It was just too terrible to imagine.

We slide down the mountain to the edge of the road. I again held them up, waiting to see if anyone saw us. Kelsey stood next to me, silently letting me make the decision of when to cross.

We'd be out in the open. If we were spotted they'd know instantly we didn't belong around here. Clenching my teeth, I nodded and we all rushed across the road and into the woods on the other side.

268

I sighed when it appeared we'd made it. "This way," I said as I led them to the south parallel to the road. We crossed a creek then finally, finally, found Papa's road. A rutted track with grass growing in the middle.

Like I said, the middle of nowhere.

My heart soared making me smile when I saw the boulder that marked the corner of Papa's property. Chase and I would always touch it when we were coming back from a hunting or fishing trip. It was our talisman. Our contact with home.

Reaching out, I rubbed my fingers along the large boulder and wondered where he was. Knowing Chase. He was up to his ears in trouble. Swallowing hard, I tried to put it out of my mind. My sister Cassie, my cousin Haley, my Dad. Where were they?

Suddenly a hope shot through me. Maybe they were already here. I mean, it was possible. Right.

"Come on, we're almost there," I said as I started to lead them up the rutted dirt road. "Fried Chicken and mashed potatoes for dinner. I promise."

My people smiled at each other. The first smile in days.

Kelsey ran to catch up to me, taking my hand. She leaned her head next to my shoulder and sighed. "I knew you'd get us here."

"Well, at least one of us knew it."

The twinkle in her eyes made my world feel wonderful. I couldn't wait for Papa to meet her. I knew the old man would love her. What is more. I think he'd be proud of me. I mean, a guy with a girl like Kelsey Morgan had to be special. Girls like her didn't attach themselves to just anybody.

We rounded a bend and came to the corner of the pasture surrounded by a split rail fence. A large sorrel horse neighed in the distance and raced across the field to check us out.

"Storm," I said as I reached over the fence to scratch his forehead. "How's it hanging? Is Cassie here?"

Kelsey joined me, petting the horse.

"Papa keeps him for Cassie and Haley." My stomach clenched up when I realized his harness looked dirty. Neither Cassie nor Haley would ever have allowed that. They weren't here."

Paul's stomach rumbled with emptiness and I remembered what was important. We kept walking. When we turned the next corner I had to stop. There it was, the farmhouse. In the yard, the large oak with the treehouse and the swing hanging beneath it.

God, how many summers had Chase and I slept up there?

The farmhouse looked the same as always. Occupying a small piece of ground cleared out of the forest. Gray clapboard siding needing a coat of paint. A thin column of smoke rising from the chimney. Beyond the house, a gray barn. A large garden on the south side, a chicken coup on the north. A dozen chickens were scratching in the dirt around the open door to the barn. Papa's old truck parked between the house and the barn.

My heart jumped. I expected him to be sitting on the porch waiting for us.

Kelsey took my hand and we started towards the house. We'd just gotten past the last fence post when my world ended. A strange man stepped out of the house, a rifle in his hands. Two more men followed him out, all of them carrying rifles, all three with pistols on their hips.

"We ain't got food," the tall leader yelled.

Kelsey gasped, squeezing my hand.

My world spun. Where was Papa? Who were these people? Then I saw it and groaned deep inside. The letters CC burned into the stock of the rifle. Papa's Rifle. I'd helped him do that the first summer we spent up here. Mom had been alive then.

"Where's Chester Conrad?" I yelled.

The tall man's brow creased. "Don't know. The place was empty. It's ours now."

The man was lying. I could tell because his lips were moving. Tall, rangy, he hadn't shaved since the asteroid hit. A scruffy beard. Jeans, and a button-down shirt. A city shirt. He wasn't from the country.

His face didn't have the wrinkled, wind-burned look of a person who spent his life outdoors. The others were pretty much the same.

The smaller guy in the back suddenly levered a round into the chamber and pointed his rifle at us. Holding it at his hip.

I froze, my shotgun was slung over my shoulder. Mrs. Carlson had my pistol. Jake was leashed. And I had women and kids I needed to keep alive.

"Okay," I said, holding up my hands. "We'll leave. Hey, no problems man."

The three men frowned, but they didn't shoot. I've got to give them credit. But it was the wrong move on their part. Because no way was I letting them keep my Papa's farm. I didn't care how many of them I had to kill.

Chapter Twenty-Three

Kelsey

My heart broke when I saw the pain in Ryan's eyes. He'd put everything into getting us here. His soul mission in life. And now. To have it taken away. Suddenly, I realized what being in love meant. It meant feeling the other person's pain at the same level. What hurt him devastated me.

I watched as his jaw clenched and I knew what was going through his mind. Just like at the ski lodge. He was having to fight to control his anger.

His grandfather wasn't here. These strange people had taken over. What did that mean for us?

I'll be honest. A worried feeling of fear ate at my stomach. This was supposed to be our salvation. But it had been taken from us. Pulled out from beneath us.

"Back off," Ryan whispered, motioning with his hand for us to back up.

I sighed inside. He wasn't going to do something crazy like take on three armed men. But what about us? I mean, it was like having the air knocked out of you. Taking any hope and desire to keep trying.

Mrs. Carlson wrapped her arms around her children and pulled them back, turning and putting herself between them and the men on the porch. Tania had to pull at Jake's leash. Mom reached out to get me going but I shrugged her off. I wasn't leaving until Ryan left.

He gently pushed at me, shooting me a quick look letting me know he was coming.

We got out of there without anyone getting shot. Our heads hung low as we shuffled around the bend and back down the road.

"Maybe a town?" Mrs. Carlson said. "They have to take us in. Women and children."

Ryan didn't answer but kept looking over his shoulder back up the road towards the farm.

"A big city," Mom said, "Or maybe the army has set up a camp."

A nervousness began to build inside of me when Ryan didn't say anything. I swear it was as if he wasn't hearing them. He'd tuned them out, his mind focused on something else.

The others kept glancing at him, wondering, worrying. He was our leader. The one who told us what we needed to do. Even the two adult women looked at him for instructions. Of course they did, they were out of their element. All of us were new to this world. But Ryan just seemed to know what to do.

He was always confident. Or at least seemed so.

Lost, I realized. He must be so lost. The last of his relatives had disappeared. His sister, his dad, his cousins. And now his grandfather. All gone. Like I said, my heart broke for him. Reaching over I tried to take his hand.

He shot me an angry scowl and pulled his hand back as he unslung his shotgun. "The road," he said, "the other side."

I frowned trying to understand but kept my mouth shut. At least he was talking. And yes, I had felt hurt when he pulled away from me. Something had changed. Didn't he feel the same about me?

Was what we had so flimsy that it could fall apart so easily?

The burning hate in his eyes made me flinch and hesitate. Seeing my shock he just pointed for me to catch up with the others.

Wow! How had this happened so fast? I was still trying to figure it all out when we reached the road. Ryan popped up, looking both ways for five minutes then motioned us across the road. We scurried over then went into the forest.

"Hold up," Ryan said, calling us back to the edge of the road on the far side from his grandfather's farm.

"No fire," he said then scoffed. "We don't have anything to cook anyway. But we can rest up here, stay out of sight."

"Why?" Paul asked.

Ryan patted the stock of his shotgun, "Because they can't get to us without crossing the road. I'd see them."

Suddenly, my heart slammed to a halt as I realized what he was thinking. "No," I gasped.

He glared at me, then back towards the farm, then asked Mrs. Carlson for the pistol.

"You are not going back there," I snapped at him.

He took a deep breath and I swear the look he gave me had the coldness of a glacier. "Kelsey, I love you with all my heart. But you're not stopping me. That was my Grandfather's rifle. They would have had to kill him to get it from him."

My jaw dropped. We hadn't discussed the L word. And now, he drops it here, in front of everyone, in front of my mom. And in the middle of a fight. So unfair. And the thought that they'd killed his grandfather was like a punch to the stomach.

"Ryan," I begged. "This is impossible. They've got rifles. There's three of them."

He ground his jaw and glared back across the road to where the farm would be. Then he sighed heavily. "We won't make it without that farm. And what happens when my sister arrives? A girl. Alone, and she runs into those three? Or my cousins."

"But, you can't."

"Kelsey, that is my family's property. My grandfather spent his life making it into something special. I'm not letting them have it. And they killed my him. No."

My insides clenched up tight as I realized there was nothing I could do to stop him.

"I'm going with you," I sighed. It was the only way I was letting this happen.

Ryan stared at me for a long moment then sighed heavily as he shook his head. "No. You're not."

An anger bubbled up inside of me. How dare he dismiss me like that. A weak woman who needed to be protected and hidden from the dangers of the world.

"Ryan. I love you," – I could do it too, drop it where he least expected it – "But if you think I am letting you face this alone. You don't know me."

He sighed then said words that still sting to this day. "Kelsey, you'll end up getting me killed."

"What?"

"Tell her," he said to my mom.

Mom held up her hands and took a step back, refusing to get into the middle of this fight. I could see it in her eyes. I was on my own.

"Kelsey," Ryan said with a heavy sigh. "If you're there, I will be more worried about protecting you than killing them. I'll make a mistake that ends up with us both dead."

I gasped. He said the word killing so easily. He had changed. Something over these last few weeks had wrestled a great part of civilization out of him. The death of his grandfather had banished the last little bit.

He was a warrior, I realized. And instinctively the warrior code had taken over. His woman needed to be protected at all costs. And his family avenged.

It was all laid out. The last weeks of fighting to survive. This new world without rules. Everything had been leading to this moment.

"Who will look after us if you're killed? When you're killed,"

He let out a long breath and shrugged. "You'll be okay. The next town, or the one after that."

Screaming, I threw up my arms in frustration.

Seeing that he had won, he smiled slightly and said, "I'll leave after dark. Mrs. Carlson, you keep the pistol. You might need it."

Glaring at him, I fought to stop from screaming at him and turned to stomp off. I needed distance as I fought to pull my emotions into some kind of control. He couldn't do this to me. Didn't I mean anything to him?

After I'd gotten a few trees between me and the others I plopped down, leaning my back next to a tree and buried my face in my hands, and cried.

It all came out. The weeks of fear, loss, and worry. All of it just erupted in an ugly cry. The worst I'd ever had. I was going to lose him. I just knew it. And I couldn't do anything to stop him.

If he loved me. Truly loved me. He wouldn't do this. Of course, I knew I was just being a baby which made me cry even more.

The tears were coming on strong when a sudden noise pulled me back. I twisted to see Julia approaching with a hesitant look. Like she'd found a baby bird in the bushes. A fledgling with no hope of a future.

She didn't say anything, instead, she sat down next to me and wrapped her arm around me.

I took a deep breath and just let her hold me for a minute then sighed heavily. It was over. I was in some kind of control again. Or at least on the edge of control.

She squeezed my shoulders then said. "He's hurting too."

"Then he shouldn't go."

"He has to," she said. "And deep down, you know he does."

"No he doesn't," I insisted. "It's his stupid pride. He can't see anything but getting back at them. He isn't thinking about the future. Our future."

She looked at me with sad eyes and shook her head. "He is who he is. We wouldn't have made it this far without him being who he is. That pride is also devotion to those he cares about. It makes him put himself between us and danger."

My insides chewed on her words. And yes, I knew she was right. I was angry at him for risking my happiness. But really, he was just being who he was. And deep down, it was why I loved him.

"When did you get so smart," I asked her as I hugged her back.

"I've been watching you for the last three weeks. You always seemed to have it together. No matter what happened. You never lost it."

"Until now," I sniffed.

She laughed. "You're justified. He can be pigheaded, can't he."

I laughed with her then suddenly realized I only had a few hours left with him and I was spending it crying in the woods. I jumped up and started back to the group.

Ryan glanced away from the road to see me coming. His brow furrowed, obviously expecting me to try and change his mind.

"Paul," I said, calling him over. "You watch for a while. They're not coming. But Ryan won't relax unless someone is watching."

Ryan frowned at me as I removed the shotgun from his hands and gave it to Paul then held out my hand for Ryan to join me.

He continued to frown, but he got up and allowed me to lead him deep into the forest. Obviously, if I only had a few hours with him. I was going to spend it alone. Just the two of us doing what people in love do, sharing ourselves, bonding ourselves together. Reminding him why I needed him to come back to me.

We were lying curled up in the blankets, my head on his chest, his arm caressing my waist, looking up through the pine bows above us at the gray sky.

"I really do love you," I said as I pulled him to me.

He squeezed then said, "Just so you know. Loving you makes me feel like my life has meaning."

Sighing, I closed my eyes and held on, praying that he would change his mind about leaving but knowing he wouldn't

We lay there until the day turned dark.

"It's time," he said as he squeezed me.

I bit my lip to stop myself from pleading with him one last time. I wouldn't do that to him. Beg, make him feel guilty. It wouldn't work and would just hurt him.

Sighing I nodded then said, "If you don't come back, I'm coming after you."

He frowned and shook his head. "If I'm not back by tomorrow afternoon. You get them down to the next town."

"No," I gasped as my insides crumbled.

He looked deep into my eyes in the fading light and said, "Kelsey, You are not to follow me. You are not to come try and rescue me. Promise me."

"No," I said as I shook my head fiercely.

He sighed heavily then said, "I need you to promise me. Please. I don't want to have to do this worried about you coming in at the wrong time."

My heart ached, he didn't want me.

"Please," he begged.

I looked up at him and knew I couldn't deny him. "I promise," I whispered.

He let out a long breath of relief and pulled me into a quick hug.

We stood there together for a long moment, taking in each other's soul. Finally, he pulled back and smiled down at me. "Come on. Your mom is going to hate me."

I frowned trying to understand then realized, I'd taken a boy into the woods for an afternoon. I smiled up at him, or at least tried to, and said, "She'll only hate you if you don't come back."

"Will you?" he asked with a concerned look in his eyes.

"No," I gasped. "Never. I will always love you. No matter what."

He sighed then said, "Words every man wants to hear. Especially from a girl like you." We hugged and walked back, arm in arm.

Ryan retrieved the shotgun, checked to make sure it was loaded, then looked at the sad faces of the group.

"You guys watch out for each other." He then gave me a quick smile and disappeared into the dark.

I waited until I was sure he was across the road then threw myself into my mother's arms and cried. I had lost him. I just knew that it would be the last time I would ever see Ryan Conrad.

Chapter Twenty-Four

Ryan

A guy with an aching heart shouldn't be sneaking through the forest determined to kill three men. His mind isn't in the right place. I kept thinking about Kelsey. The way her body felt. The soft smell of coconut. How her voice seemed to soothe my soul.

God, I loved her so much. But she just didn't understand. I had to get our farm back. We wouldn't survive without it. We might not survive anyway, but it was our best chance.

I could see our new world laid out in front of us. Little food. Roving bands of desperate people. A government that would crack down, picking winners and losers. Our only hope was to disappear. Not interact with others and hope to be forgotten.

To do that. We needed my grandfather's farm. Hopefully, we would be able to grow enough food for ourselves.

A sick doubt filled me. All this rain, it was time for spring planting but the ground was soggy. And I swear I had barely seen the sun in three weeks. What if it stayed like this forever?

And, how was I supposed to plant a field of wheat or corn? Did Papa have seed? And we didn't have the tools. I mean, how was I supposed to make a horse-drawn plow?

Nervousness wiggled through me as I thought about how much I didn't know. In the back of my mind had been the knowledge that Papa would be there. And he knew everything. Now I was alone.

This new burden on my shoulders felt like a crushing weight.

Grinding my teeth, I pushed my self-doubts out of my mind and focused on the burning hate. These men had killed my grandfather. A man I loved, respected, needed. They'd taken my family from me and threatened the lives of those I loved.

The thought of Kelsey and the others dying on the side of the road made me want to hurt someone. A burning needed at the bottom of my stomach drove me to put my fist through someone's chest and pull their heart out.

I know, melodramatic. But it was how I felt. I mean literally.

"Careful, boy," I mumbled to myself. My cousin Chase used to tease me, saying I had gotten the calm gene, and they'd doubled up on the pissed-off gene for him. But my heart was pounding so hard I couldn't reach a calmness.

Stopping just the other side of the road I took a deep breath. The air smelled of pine and moldy needles. A gentle breeze came in from the north with a hint of rain. The air tickling my skin.

"Think this through," I mumbled to myself. I did this when I needed to stop myself from reacting too fast. Talked to myself. And it worked. The anger began to change over to determination as I began to plan.

The clouds moved back in, the night was getting darker. That inside a cupboard dark. I had to work my way slowly with the barrel of the shotgun leading the way to make sure I didn't run into a tree branch.

An hour later, when I got to the farm I pulled back. The open space let in enough light to barely see the outline of the house and barn.

"Now what?" I whispered as I examined the place. I could sneak in, shoot them in their sleep. A sick feeling of doubt worried me. What if I hesitated at the last moment? What if one of them was up and shot me before I got a chance?

The thought of leaving Kelsey and the others all alone ate at my stomach with a gnawing hunger.

No, there were three of them. I'd never get them all if I went in. So that meant picking them off one at a time. I had something they didn't. Time, surprise, patience.

Suddenly a light flashed inside the house as someone lit a lantern. My grandfather's storm lanterns, I thought as I ground my back teeth.

The light through the curtains was enough to see details. Their night vision will be shot. One point in my favor.

I studied the situation then dropped to my belly and began to crawl. I would work my way to behind the barn. Between it and the chicken coop would give me an excellent view and some cover.

The wet ground soaked through me, making me smell of mud and grass as I moved on my belly like I'd seen a hundred soldiers do in all those movies. Keep low, don't let them see me, I had all the time in the world. Make them come to me.

Finally, I reached the corner of the barn then suddenly ran into a long pile of fresh earth. My stomach dropped as I realized what it was. My grandfather's grave. They'd buried him behind the barn.

I gulped back a tear and whispered. "I'll make them pay, Papa, I promise."

Sadness filled me. Oh, how I wished he would have met Kelsey. I wanted to see the look of approval in his eyes. A thousand memories flashed through my mind. The first time he taught me his special knot for fishing hooks. The long lazy summer nights we had sat up playing 42, or when I was real little, he'd bounced me and Cassie on his knee and sighed with pure happiness.

I'd loved him, always. That unconditional love a child has for a grandparent. And now he had been murdered by these men.

"No mercy," I hissed under my breath and worked my way around the barn to watch the house. I'd wait, the chickens were penned up for the night, someone would have to come let them out in the morning. I'd take him then.

Settling in, I pulled my jacket close and waited.

Throughout the night, I thought of Kelsey, Papa, my sister, my cousins, my dad. And my Mom. Oh, how I missed her. A part of me was glad she had missed all of this. She would have been so terrified of her children being hurt.

Sighing, I wiggled to get more comfortable and waited. Kelsey, Wow, who would have thought? A girl like her falling in love with me. I smiled to myself when I remembered the shock on her face when I said I loved her. A surprised look was quickly followed by an ecstatic look of happiness, almost immediately followed by anger as she returned to our fight.

"You'll never be boring," I said to the night.

Storm stomping in the barn woke me. My eyes shot open as I froze, terrified I'd screwed up. The sky was beginning to turn purple in the east. Had I slept? Could they already be sneaking up on me?

No, I realized. They didn't need to sneak. I'd been out like a light, they could have driven up in a tank and killed me in my sleep.

Sighing, I took a deep breath and refocused on the house as I tried to forgive myself for falling asleep. I mean, I'd barely eaten in three weeks. It'd gotten so bad, that my belt buckle was becoming good friends with my spine.

As the sky grew lighter, I moved back to the corner of the barn, peeking around the edge.

"Come on," I mumbled to myself as my muscles ached, needing to be released into action. My finger caressed the trigger. "Come on, you bastards."

I had almost given up when the front door cracked and the youngest guy stepped out, stretching, scratching at his lower back. Taking a deep breath, he jumped off the porch and started for the coop.

No gun, I realized as I smiled. No, why would he need one? They'd scared off the weirdos from the day before.

Hawking in the back of his throat he spit to the side then jumped to get around a puddle.

Closer, I thought to myself. I could shoot him without warning and he'd die before he hit the ground. But the others would be warned. Instead, I had a plan. And sure enough, he did as I expected,

The door to the coop was on the far side, away from the house. And like I thought, he opened the door and stepped in to get any eggs. I gripped the shotgun so tightly that my knuckles were white even in the weak light.

I bent at the waist as I slipped in next to the door and waited.

A moment later he stepped out, his hands cradling six eggs.

I learned something that day. A shotgun's butt up next to a man's head makes a strange sound. A cross between a thwack and a thud.

He crumpled to the ground, breaking the eggs.

I stared down at him, the shotgun raised, ready to strike again. But there wasn't a need. He was out. A small dent at the temple will do that to a person.

Letting out a long breath I watched his chest rise. He wasn't dead. Not yet. But I needed him out of the way. I grabbed his collar and dragged him into the barn through the back door that opened to the paddock.

Smiling to myself I shook my head as I saw Papa's ball of plastic twine in the corner. The twine used to bind the haybales. He would wrap it all up together until the ball got too big then dump it at a recycling place in town.

I snatched a couple of five-foot sections then tied up my prisoner, making sure not to be too gentle. Hands behind his back, tied to his ankles. The guy wasn't going anywhere. Then I stuffed an old oily rag in his mouth and tied it off.

Finally, I tied him to a post and stepped back, looking for anything I might have missed.

He was still out, and, I'll be honest, I didn't really care if he ever came too. The only reason I hadn't killed him already was because I didn't want to make the noise.

I tossed an armful of hay to Storm then sneaked out the back and around to the corner to wait.

A good twenty minutes later the second guy stepped out of the house. Heavy set, a pistol on his hip. He held a hand to his forehead and searched for his friend. "Bobby," he yelled.

I smiled and waited.

Cursing under his breath he stepped off the porch and started for the coop.

I held my breath waiting. But he didn't go for the chickens, instead, twisting and starting for the barn. He'd see my prisoner. Swallowing, I stepped out and held up my shotgun, yelling for him to freeze.

He slammed to a halt, his eyes growing to the size of pumpkins, unable to look away from that twelve gauge pointing at his gut.

I swear, it was taking every bit of control not to pull the trigger when my world spun out of control as something slammed into my leg, knocking me to the ground.

Third guy, the leader, had stepped out onto the porch and shot me.

Second guy reacted fast, pulling his pistol like he was an old-fashioned cowboy, and started to fire, the slug kicking up dirt in front of my face.

I didn't think, I just pointed and pulled the trigger. The blast caught him square in the gut, knocking him back six feet. I knew if he wasn't dead already he soon would be.

Suddenly, another shot rang out from the porch and I felt a burning sensation down my arm.

A feeling of failure filled me. I'd screwed this up. I should have just gone in there and shot them in their sleep. My leg screamed at me in roaring pain as I rolled out of the way and back behind the corner of the barn.

Two more shots exploded in the morning, both ripping chunks of wood off the barn as he put out searching fire.

My mind scrambled as I tried to figure out what to do. My leg was bleeding like a stuck pig. But no pulsing, just a solid leak. Setting my shotgun aside I pulled over a piece of twine and wrapped it around my upper thigh then used a stick to twist it into a tourniquet.

Stay alive, I told myself. Just stay alive long enough to kill him. Kelsey and the others could live in peace. But only if the bastard was dead.

Gritting my teeth, I snuck a look around the edge of the barn. Second guy was lying in the dirt where my blast had put him. But third guy was gone. My gut tightened. He could be anywhere. And a rifle could stand off and pluck me whenever he wanted.,

Using the shotgun as a crutch, I pulled myself up and worked to the front edge of the barn, I needed to know where he was at. What direction he was coming from?

The cool morning air bit at the back of my throat as a taste of metal filled my mouth. A dizziness hit me and I knew I was losing too much blood. Even if I did get this guy by some miracle, I probably wouldn't make it. Not in this new world. There were no ambulances. And no phones to call one. No police to come racing to my rescue. No doctors to sew me back together.

I took a deep breath and stuck my head further around the corner to get a better look. Nothing. I was turned to go back and work my way around to the other side when the world exploded again as I was knocked to the ground.

A million stars erupted around me as I fought to bring my shotgun up. I think the only thing that saved me was him having problems with the bolt. He jerked it back too hard, too fast, and got it caught. He was fighting to get another round in the chamber when my shotgun exploded.

I don't remember pulling the trigger. But I do remember him being lifted up to fall back onto the ground, his sightless eyes stared up at the gray sky.

Closing my eyes, I fought to remain conscious. I needed to get back. Kelsey needed to know it was safe. They could stay here. A sudden worry filled me. I didn't get back. They left for the town to never return. Their haven lost.

A sick dread filled me as I hobbled across the yard. Fighting to get a breath as my world began to spin.

I wasn't going to make it I realized just as I collapsed and the world went dark.

Chapter Twenty-Five

Kelsey

The longest night of my life was spent curled up next to my mother under a tarp in the trees as I silently cried to myself and all I had lost.

I knew Ryan would be furious with me if I followed him. I was going to go anyway but then I remembered his words. I'd just get him killed. I'd be in the wrong place at the wrong time and he'd make a mistake that cost him his life.

I'd never be able to live with myself.

No, I had to trust him. A boy I barely knew. A boy I loved with all my heart. A boy who might be dead at any moment.

How had my life become so messed up? Three weeks earlier, I was worried about cheer practice. Who would ask me to Prom? What if no one asked? Should I go alone? You know, serious stuff.

Now, I could only wait. A long, soul-crushing wait.

"He'll be fine," Mom said as she rubbed my back.

I scoffed and turned on her, how dare she say that? She didn't believe it.

"No," I growled. "he's going to get killed and I can't save him."

My mom sighed as she put her arm around me, trying to comfort me but there was nothing she could do. Nobody could fix this but Ryan.

When the birds began to twirp and the sky was lighting, I sat up and crawled out from beneath the tarp and stared towards the farm. Please I begged. I'll be the best person possible I pleaded, just bring him back to me.

Suddenly, a rifle shot echoed off the mountains behind us.

My stomach clenched as I fell to my knees. A rifle, not a shotgun. Was he dead? Then I heard the shotgun and my heart soared. He was fighting back.

Without thinking I started towards him but Mom grabbed my arm and said, "No. You can't."

I could see the fear in her eyes. Her baby was about to charge into a gunfight.

Two more rifle shots made me twitch.

"You're Mom's right," Paul said with a sad look. "You don't know what is happening. You might make it worse."

"He needs me," I said as I stared towards the sound.

Both Mrs. Carlson and Mom put their hands on my arms, holding me back. I don't know what I would have done but another rifle shot followed by a shotgun blast just tore my heart out at the roots.

"I can't," I screamed at them then twisted and jumped to get past them. "Keep Jake here," I yelled over my shoulder as I raced across the road without checking if it was clear. All I could think about was Ryan dying without me.

I was halfway up the dirt road when I slid to a stop and thought. Don't get him killed, I told myself as I couldn't force myself forward.

The silence ate into me. No more shots. Was he already dead? Or were they both hiding, waiting for the first one to move? Would me showing up make Ryan step out and get him killed?

A fearful dread filled me. What should I do? He needed me. I just knew it. But I couldn't go to him.

Suddenly, without thinking, I turned off into the forest. I'd come in from behind, I thought. Ryan wouldn't see me. The other men wouldn't see me. I could just get close enough to find out what was going on. What I could do to help?

The morning light was just bright enough so I could weave my way between the trees. Please, I kept begging over and over. Still be alive. My stomach rolled with fear. I couldn't lose him. I just couldn't.

When the edge of the forest came into sight I slowed down and gingerly stepped forward to peek out.

My heart fell. A man lay in the dirt between the house and the barn. His corpse a tangled mess. Ryan? "No, please no."

Slowly I saw the jean jacket stained with blood and realized it wasn't Ryan. My heart began to beat again.

Where? I scanned the area, wanting to call out to him, terrified I'd make things worse. Stuck between impossible and hopeless. Finally, I took a deep breath and walked along the edge of the forest, staying just inside the trees.

I had just gotten to where I could see behind the barn and saw a second man, also dead. Unbelievable, Ryan had gotten two of them. But where was he? My heart refused to slow down as I rushed forward.

He had to be somewhere. I couldn't take it anymore. I had to find him. I had to know.

As I passed the man behind the barn I saw the rifle lying next to him. The one Ryan had told me belonged to his grandfather. I paused to make sure he was dead. But a person doesn't survive that much damage.

Swallowing hard I started around the side of the barn and saw him. My Ryan, lying face down in the dirt.

"No," I yelled. Thoughts about the third man were not a thing. All I could see was Ryan, dead or dying.

"Ryan," I yelled as I dropped down next to him, my heart racing, my eyes blurred with misty tears. "Please, Ryan," I begged as I touched him, afraid to move him but desperate to know. A nasty wound along the side of his head made my stomach rebel. There was another on his arm, and his leg looked like someone had poked a steel bar through it.

"Ryan," I said softly as I gently felt his neck, desperate, terrified, numb with fear. "Please," I whispered.

My fingers trembled as I held them next to his neck, waiting, was I doing this right, or was he dead? No pulse. No, this couldn't be happening.

"Ryan," I yelled as I pushed him over onto his back. I lowered my ear to his chest, holding my breath so I could hear the faintest sound.

Suddenly, I felt his chest rise as he took a breath.

"Oh, Ryan," I cried as tears fell onto the muddy ground like a leaking hose.

He was alive. I couldn't believe it, he was still alive. Every good thing that had happened in my life was nothing compared to that moment. The sense of relief and hope was almost too much.

Bending down, I hugged him, refusing to ever let him go.

"You're hurting me," he grunted.

I freaked and backed away, staring at him, unable to believe he was awake.

"What should I do?" I asked as I fumbled to figure it out. I was so messed up inside, it was like I'd become an idiot all of a sudden, unable to think, unable to understand.

He sighed and closed his eyes and I knew I'd lost him again. He was unconscious. When I saw his chest rise again I started yelling "Mom, Mom," as I ran back toward them. I'm not proud that I couldn't do this by myself and I hated leaving him. But I'd have done anything if it made sure he lived.

They raced across the road before I got there. "He's alive," I gasped as I bent at the waist to get enough air. "Barely."

The others started running up the dirt road. Tania released Jake so he could race ahead. We found him licking Ryan's face.

"Let's get him inside," Mom said. It took us all working together to get Ryan up onto the porch and into the house. Julia ran forward then ran back and said, "The room on the right."

Somewhere in the back of my mind, I heard Paul say something about the third man, grab the shotgun and leave us. None of it registered. All that mattered was Ryan.

It took me and Mom an hour to get him sort of fixed. Mrs. Carlson found first aid supplies. Tania brought us kitchen scissors to cut off his clothing. Jake sat next to the bed watching us work, making sure we did a good job.

Only after we had him all bandaged and tucked into bed did I look around and take it all in. We were here, finally, and Ryan was still alive. Sinking to my knees, I laid my head on the bed next to him praying like I'd never prayed before. Promising my soul if he'd only live.

Mom gently pulled me back and said, "Let him rest. They've found food."

I was too numb to shrug her off and allowed her to guide me out of the room. The house was large with a kitchen and dining room facing a living room. Three bedrooms in the back. But it all just barely registered. All I could think about was Ryan.

"You won't believe it," Julia said, "Ryan was right. The cellar is full of food. There must be a thousand jars. Bags of flour."

It didn't register. We were safe, and none of it really mattered unless Ryan lived.

Mrs. Carlson had made a quick stew on the gas stove and placed a bowl in front of me. My stomach squeezed with need but I couldn't force myself to eat. Suddenly the front door burst open and Paul pulled a man in, his hands and feet tied.

"Found him," Paul said. "Ryan had him tied up in the barn."

An anger filled me. This was my enemy. A man who had tried to kill Ryan. I jumped up and raced towards him, my hands up, determined to claw his eyes out.

"No," Paul said as he stepped in front to hold me off.

I swatted at him to get at my enemy. But Paul held me, whispering, "Ryan wouldn't want this."

"I'll kill him," I yelled as I faked left then deaked right, Paul shifted and I was clear. The man's eyes were filled with fear as he tried to back away from me.

"Kelsey," a deep voice called and in the back of my head, a strange awareness registered. Turning I saw Ryan wrapped in a blanket leaning against the wall, his pale face staring at me, pleading. "Enough killing."

My heart filled with love as I saw him give me a small smile. "Besides, I don't want my children knowing their mother killed a man. It sets a bad example."

Everything disappeared except for the man I loved. The man I would always love.

Epilogue

Kelsey

A nervousness filled me. Ryan was sitting on the porch, staring out at the rain. Mom caught the fear in my eyes and said, "He is going to be fine. He might limp. But he'll be fine. He's come so far in this last month."

"He's going to leave me," I said. "To find his sister."

"Maybe," Mom said with a heavy sigh. "But it won't be for months. Not until he can walk better. And a lot can happen between then and now."

I bit my lip as I looked at him through the window and felt my heart melt. It always did when I looked at him. He'd saved us so many times. Leaving Mom, I stepped out onto the porch and sat down next to him on the bench. "What are you thinking about?"

He gave me a quick smile then said. "We need to get a garden in. four or five. A field of potatoes, or corn. Something to get us through next winter. But this rain. I don't know."

I sighed, that was so my Ryan, always thinking about what to do next. "Are you also thinking about your sister?"

He glanced at me then took a deep breath and nodded. "I know she's down in Oklahoma. Or was when this started. But she could be anywhere. The same for Haley in New York. Or Chase in California. How do I find them?"

"Maybe we wait until they come here," I said, as I fought to hold down the rising hope deep inside of me.

He just sighed and said, "We'll see."

Snugling in next to him I laid my head on his shoulder and thought about my secret. I couldn't tell him yet. I wasn't sure. But something told me it was true. My body just felt different. Would he be happy? How could we bring a child into this world? But deep in my heart, I knew this was right. That Ryan would be the best father. That the world needed to keep going and children, our children, would make it all worthwhile.

A thousand fears filled me. Food, raiders, what if his family didn't like me? I cold shiver ran down my back as I thought about them all fighting to get here. We were their best chance. Would they make it? Please, I thought. My man deserved them. All we could do was wait, and hope.

Suddenly, Jake barked, the fur on his back at full force. We looked and saw, two people walking towards us. A very tall man, his arm in a sling, with a golden retriever on a leash, and a young woman holding something in her arms..

Once again, my world was put on hold.

The End

Author's Afterword

I do hope you enjoyed the novel. My last series explored what happens when everyone dies, and technology is lost. This time, I wanted to explore what happens when Technology is lost resulting in everyone dying. Again, the important question, what would I do in that situation.

I have often wondered what would happen if my family was separated by great distance when the world ended?

As always, I wish to thank friends who have helped, authors Erin Scott, and Anya Monroe. And my special friend Sheryl Turner. But most of all I want to thank my wife Shelley for all she puts up with. It can be difficult being an author's spouse. We have a tendency to live in our own little worlds. Our minds drifting to strange new places, keeping us unaware of what is happening around us. Thankfully I am married to a woman who knows when to let me write and knows when to pull me back into the real world.

If you liked this story. I hope to have the next book in the series out in a few months. In the mean time, I have put in a small sample of the first book in my other series, The End of Everything (The End of Everything 1) truly believe you would enjoy it.

Thank you again

Nate Johnson

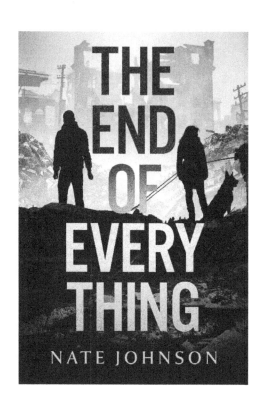

THE END OF EVERY THING

NATE JOHNSON

The End of Everything

Chapter One

Nick

I didn't say goodbye to my mom that day. A fact that I would regret on my deathbed. Being an angry seventeen-year-old was my only excuse. It was my mom who sent me away. Her way of stopping me from becoming an even worse jerk.

A boy gets in one fight and the world comes crashing down on him. Granted, breaking a guy's arm and knocking out a couple of teeth for the other one made it seem worse. But then they had it coming, believe me.

Anyway, Mom figured six weeks as a Counselor in Training at Camp Tecumseh in Eastern Pennsylvania would keep me away from bad influences. A nice peaceful summer she said. God, how wrong could a person be?

But like I said, I didn't even turn to look at her when I stepped up onto the bus. If I'd known I'd never see her again, I might have given a damn. I might not have been such a jerk. At least I like to think so. It's how I keep from beating myself up about it.

I nodded to the driver. The same guy I remembered from my camp five years earlier. Then Dad died and going away to summer camp became an unnecessary expense. But Mom thought it would be good for me to do this CIT thing. It didn't cost anything. Free labor. So here I was on a bus to hell.

It was a day before the camp was supposed to start so this was just for the early birds. The kids and CITs that couldn't show up tomorrow. Nine kids and two girl CITs. Tomorrow there would be a hundred and forty campers arriving along with twenty CITs and staff.

Being the typical boy, I checked out the girls immediately. Both about my age, maybe sixteen. The one on the right had long brown hair in a ponytail. Pretty, with discerning eyes. Something told me, rich girl. I don't know. Maybe it was just the attitude.

The one on the left. Shorter, blond, with glasses. Pretty but not as much as ponytail.

I knew what they saw when they looked back at me. A tall guy with a scowl. I had a habit of standing out in a crowd. A fact that always bugged me at my core. I wasn't lanky. More solid. But tall. Six three and I wouldn't see eighteen for another two months.

The rest of the bus had nine kids, eleven to twelve years old, spread out. Five girls and four boys. They were looking at me with

315

shaded frowns. Was I the typical jerk or a special one?

Shifting my backpack on my shoulder, I made my way down the aisle to the end then jerked my thumb for the kid in the back seat to move.

The kid had the good sense to scurry out of the seat.

I plopped down and stared into nothing.

The driver pushed the bus into gear, and we were off. Six weeks I thought. I could do anything for six weeks. It wasn't the end of the world.

Ha, that always makes me laugh. When it comes to being mistaken. No person had ever been more wrong.

The bus crawled through the small town and then started up a switch-back two-lane road into the mountains. I stared out the window at the forest and occasional farm of the Pocono Mountains. Not much different than the area around Syracuse, I thought.

Six weeks I reminded myself. I guess it was better than jail, even if only slightly.

A little over an hour and we finally got there, about twenty-five miles out from the town. I guess this place was farther out than I remembered. When you are a little kid, you don't pick up on things like that. But we were finally there, and things hadn't changed one bit.

About twenty cabins clustered on the far end of the lake. Four main buildings up on a hill above the lake and cabins. On the left, the admin building. Built of thick logs. Next, the combined mess hall and kitchen. Then the showers and restrooms. If I remembered correctly divided down the middle with six showers and eight cubicles on each side. It got busy in the morning, to say the least. And finally, the staff building. More like a dormitory.

Everything was as I remembered it. Even the same float sat in the middle of the lake.

I almost smiled to myself when I remembered the first time, I had swum all the way out there in a race with Billy Jenkins. I wondered where he was. Probably hanging out with his friends, playing video games, or a pick-up basketball game. Things I would end up never knowing. Billy was lost to history. As if he never lived.

I wonder if he'd been playing video games when it all ended. Fighting off monsters while invisible ones ate him up from the inside.

Three sailboats were moored to a pier sticking out into the lake, their sails furled and stowed. The large firepit off to the side looked like it was all ready for hotdogs and smores.

It was the first warm day of summer late spring day. A little cooler up here in the mountains with a high blue sky. But it was the smell though that told me I was somewhere different. A green smell filled with life. Or maybe it was the absence of car exhaust and wet asphalt. Anyway, I took a deep breath and almost relaxed. Then I remembered I was angry at the world and pushed it aside.

The blond and ponytail were waiting for me. The driver Thompson or Thomas or something was rounding up the kids and said he'd be back for us in a minute. The blond stepped forward with a wide smile and I knew the type immediately. She would want to be friends. For life even.

"I'm Brie Osborn," she said holding out her hand.

I shook it, making sure not to apply too much pressure. Mom had gone out of her way to try and make a gentleman out of me. For the most part, she had failed, but some things stuck.

"And this is Jenny," she said indicating the pony-haired girl.

"Jennifer," the girl corrected as she held out her hand.

Again, I made a point of not squeezing too hard. For the briefest moment we stared into each other's eyes, and I saw it immediately. She didn't like me. To her, I was a bug that had dropped onto her plate of food.

I don't know what I'd done. And really, it didn't matter. She wouldn't be the first pretty girl who didn't think I was worth a damn.

Letting go of her hand, I turned away to look out over the camp. Six weeks, I reminded myself and then I was out of here. Two groups of snot-nosed kids to be shepherded.

As I stood there, an awkward silence fell over the three of us. I wanted to smile. They were pretty girls and weren't used to being ignored. But no way was I getting interested. Well, at least not officially.

Thankfully the awkward silence was broken by Thompson returning. He was the manager, I reminded myself. He'd been running this place for years. He had everything down to a system if I remembered correctly. A tight timetable that kept everyone too busy to get into trouble.

I wondered if he knew about me. There had been a police report. But the charges had been dropped when they finally figured out the two other guys were even worse jerks than me. No. He didn't I realized. He would never have accepted Mom's application.

Oh, well. No need to inform him of my past. I'd do my time then go home to finish out my senior year and then off to start some kind of life that I still hadn't figured out.

That memory. Standing there, thinking about the future hurts now. More than you will ever know.

Thompson returned after showing the kids their cabin. He had to be in his late forties with a bit of a paunch. A gray sweatshirt with Camp Tecumseh across the chest and a Yankee's ball cap that looked like it had been dunked in the lake a dozen times.

"Make sure they feel comfortable. Stop the arguments over who gets which bunk. You know stuff like that. Then have them up at the mess hall by five."

Jenny frowned at him. I had determined that I would refer to her as Jenny just to piss her off. "Aren't there any counselors? I thought we were supposed to be learning. You know the whole 'in training' part of things."

The old man had a brief worried look then shook his head. "A couple of them were supposed to show up today. But they got delayed. They'll be here tomorrow along with the rest."

Jenny decided not to push the issue but picked up her backpack and started down the hill. Obviously, she knew where she was going. If I had to guess, I bet she'd been a camper here for ten years and was going through this CIT stuff so she could get on staff next year.

As she walked down the hill, I had to admit her butt was way above average in jeans that were just the right amount of tight.

Thompson caught me checking her out and shook his head before slapping my shoulder. "Don't even think about it."

I laughed for the first time in two weeks. That was going to be an impossibility. I was a seventeen-year-old boy. That was all I thought about.

The blond, Brie, I reminded myself, hurried to catch up with her friend.

Old man Thompson showed me the boy's CIT cabin. On the opposite side of the camp from the girl's CIT cabin. With eighteen cabins for the campers between them. Obviously, these people weren't stupid.

I threw my stuff onto the farthest of eight bunks and wondered what the other CITs would be like. I shrugged my shoulders. I wasn't here to make lifetime friends.

Okay, it couldn't be avoided any longer. I found the cabin with the four boys and entered without knocking. You would have thought that a werewolf had stepped into the place. All four froze, looking at me with wide eyes.

I could see it instantly. Like all boys. At some point in their life they had been bullied by older, bigger boys. The natural instinct was to freeze in the presence of a predator.

Scanning them I saw the usual. Kids. The smallest in the back frowned, but I had to give him credit, he didn't look away.

"I'm Nick," I told them. "I'm supposed to make sure you guys don't get lost on the way to the mess hall. Any problems I need to solve? ... Good. Finish up."

They scrambled to make up their bunks. Sheets and blankets had been left on each one. Once that was done I had them put their stuff away in lockers. They still had that haunted look, waiting for things to go wrong.

"God, lighten up guys," I said. "I won't screw with you. Not unless you deserve it. What are your names?"

"Mike," a chunky kid with red hair said then bit his tongue, obviously wondering if that was the right answer. "Mike Jackson."

Okay. I know I can be intimidating. My size, the fresh scar over my left eyebrow. Oh yeah, and the permanent scowl.

"Carl, Carl Bender," a lanky black kid. Okay, if we had a basketball tournament, I was picking him for my team.

"Anthony, but I prefer Tony. Tony Gallo," A dark-haired Italian kid said as he pushed his glasses back up to the bridge of his nose.

I nodded then turned to the last one. The smallest, and probably youngest. "And you."

The kids finished putting his stuff away, hesitated, then said "Patterson Abercrombie."

The other boys laughed, and I saw the pain shoot behind the kid's eyes. I wondered how many times that had happened in his life and how many times it would in the future. Of course, we all ended up having way worse futures than people laughing at our names. But I didn't know that then so I did what anyone would have done and laughed along with everyone else, but I followed it up by saying, "That's too hard to remember. Besides, a name like that makes you sound like a stockbroker, and you look too intelligent to ever fall into that scam. So I'm going to call you … Bud. That okay?"

The kid's eyes grew big, and I knew he'd never had a nickname in his entire life. At least not one he liked. Smiling, he nodded.

"Okay," I said as I examined them. "Mike, Carl, Tony, and Bud. God, it sounds like a boy band. You guys break out singing and I'll disown you. I swear."

They laughed and the tension was broken. I wasn't a special jerk, perhaps only a regular one and they could live with that.

Oh, if we had but known what a person could live with and without.

Chapter Two

Jenifer

Camp Tecumseh, God, I loved it. The one place in the world that was safe. Safe from overprotective parents and a judgmental world. No maids reporting to mom every time I broke the slightest rule. I swear I think she paid them extra for every time they ratted me out. Here I could be me. Jennifer O'Brien.

The smells, the colors, the soft breeze. All of it brought back fond memories. And now, finally, I was a CIT. Everything was how it was supposed to be. CIT this summer. Then senior at school next year. After that, either Harvard or Yale. My parents were still arguing about which. But none of that mattered. I was at Camp Tecumseh for the next six weeks and my future was bright.

HA! What a crock of ... stuff that turned out to be.

When we reached the CIT cabin I turned and looked back at that boy going into his cabin. Well, nothing could be perfect. All I could do was shake my head. This Nick person was so wrong for Camp Tecumseh.

I knew the type only too well. A bad boy to his very core. It was obvious, the heavy scowl, the wide shoulders, denim jacket, and the way he talked. As if everyone else in the world was without value. Yes, A definite bad boy.

Unlike most other girls. Bad boys did nothing for me. No fluttering butterflies. No halted breath. No, they were a waste with no socially redeeming value. Especially here.

Deep down, I knew the problem was that he reminded me of my dad. That same cocky attitude and that inability to be faithful. Mom might forgive my dad, but I still couldn't.

Brie glanced to where I was looking and smiled. "It is going to be an interesting summer."

I laughed and shook my head. "Let's hope not. Don't forget. We are here to keep the peace and make sure nothing bad happens."

Well, we failed at that, didn't we? Or at least the world did.

After Brie and I got settled we headed over to the girl's cabin. Brie and I had known each other for eight years. Not bosom buddies. But we'd shared a cabin a couple of times. Been on the same tug-a-war teams that type of thing.

When we got to the girl's cabin we knocked and waited to be let in. Five young girls. Three of them had been here before. The other two were newbies, watching the others to see what to do next.

I was pleased to see bunks being made and things put away in lockers. Eleven and twelve year old's. God, I remembered that awful time of being in between. No longer child, not yet woman. I smiled to myself. It was why girls this age formed such tight bonds with each other. They were the only ones who truly understood.

"I'm Jennifer, this is Brie. We're here if you need any help. Answer any questions."

The five girls stared back, some shrugging before returning to finish their work. I couldn't help but smile. Brie and I were already outsiders. We might be used for information, but we weren't one of them.

An hour on a bus and a shared cabin and they were already forming a team to face the world. After introductions, I watched them for a moment and immediately started putting them into categories.

Ashley Chan, Asian-American. A quick smile and a born helper. She was already assisting Katy Price in finishing with her bunk.

Katy Price, brunet, shy. When I saw her slip a Harry Potter book into her locker I had to smile. Only a true bookworm brings a book to camp. I knew she would have preferred to lay in the shade of a tree and read instead of swimming or games. No, for her, other worlds were her fascination.

Then there was Nicole Parsons. She was easy to figure out. A hint of eyeshadow and lip gloss. Twelve going on sixteen. With a hint of toughness behind her eyes. Nicole was the type of person you didn't want to get on the wrong side of.

Emma Davis, a strawberry blond was watching everyone else with a keen eye. A newbie, she had a natural curiosity. The diary sitting on top of her upper bunk confirmed it. She'd chronicle every detail. Locking onto paper what she couldn't remember.

And finally, Harper Reed. The other first-timer. Confident, not needing to watch the others to know what to do. Tall, pretty on her way to being beautiful. A future heartbreaker. Supermodel in training. A sketchbook slipped under her mattress exposed the secret to her soul. An artist. I wondered if she was any good. Yes, I thought. There was something about Harper that said she would be good at anything she did.

Five young girls. My responsibility. At least until the counselors showed up.

I shook my head. They really should have been here already, getting ready. I was disappointed in them. It was just plain wrong to treat Camp as unimportant. Of course, now it is hard to blame people for being late when they were in the process of dying. It seems sort of petty, if you know what I mean.

After getting everyone settled, we headed up to the mess hall for dinner. The seven of us went through the line for salad, garlic bread, and spaghetti. Not my favorite, but that was the thing about Camp food. You ate what they served, or you went without.

We all sat at a table off to the right. Talking, sharing, an occasional giggle. When the boys showed up, the feeling in the room changed. I couldn't help but shake my head. Even at this young age, the girls were very aware of boys being in the vicinity.

Of course the male members of our species were typical, loud, and rambunctious, with someone throwing a punch at another's shoulder. It was almost as if they were trying to draw attention to themselves. The four of them got their meals and made it a point of sitting as far away as possible.

They wanted attention but didn't want to get contaminated by girls.

Then there was that Nick person. God, what a cold, non-caring, waste of oxygen. He stepped up and Mrs. Smith, the cook, smiled at him as if he were special then gave him a double serving without him having to ask. And of course he skipped the salad entirely.

But it was when he sat down all alone, separate from the boys that I saw his true self. A loner. Most definitely not Camp Tecumseh material. Oh, well, it was only six weeks.

Again, HA!

The next morning was pretty much the same thing only pancakes instead of spaghetti. It had been a restless night. The newness was already wearing off. The girls had probably stayed up half the night sharing stories about where they were from. Now it was simply a matter of waiting for the other campers to show up so we could get started.

I was trying to organize a volleyball game when Mr. Thompson and Mrs. Smith stepped out of the admin building and called, Brie, myself, and Nick over. The camp manager had a deep frown and kept looking to the front gate. Mrs. Smith simply shook her head.

My stomach clenched up just a bit. I knew that look. It was the look my father got when things didn't go the way he expected. It was just a matter of figuring out who to blame.

"There seems to be a problem," he said with a shake of his head.

The three of us stood there waiting. This could be anything from rat poison in the pancake batter to someone forgetting to order enough toilet paper.

I couldn't help but notice that the Nick person didn't frown. I swear the man could have been told he was to die in an hour, and he wouldn't have cared one way or the other.

"It seems," Mr. Thompson continued. "That some of the staff are still delayed. Mrs. Smith will have to drive the other bus."

It was a little confusing, how did he know they weren't arriving. I knew from long experience that there was no cell coverage up here. Then I suddenly realized that as a result of the changes he meant that there weren't going to be any adults left.

"You guys will have to keep an eye on things."

Okay, I could live with that. A bit better than rat poison.

"Nick, you'll be in charge. Keep them away from the lake and the forest. It will only be a couple of hours."

Mr. Bad boy nodded, as if it was no big deal, being left in charge. I of course wanted to scream, how come he got picked? But I had learned long ago not to challenge older men. It was a waste of time, they never saw reason. My father being a prime example.

"There is stuff to make sandwiches," Mrs. Smith said, "If we're not back in time for lunch. But no using the stove and stay out of the ice cream. That is for special circumstances."

That last line makes me want to both laugh and cry. I'll tell you about it when we get to that part of the story.

Mr. Thompson stared at the front gate for a minute and shook his head Then took a deep breath and nodded for Mrs. Smith to follow him.

We three CITs were joined by the nine campers and stood there to watch the two big yellow buses drive through the front gate.

I think that is the point where my story started. Really. There was my life before and my life after. A life in what used to be the normal world and this life. Believe me, they aren't the same. Not even close.

The End of Everything (The End of Everything 1)

Made in the USA
Coppell, TX
26 November 2024

41069146R00184